# STOLEN MIDSUMMER BRIDE

## STOLEN BRIDES OF THE FAE

### TARA GRAYCE

Sword & Cross
Publishing

*For Buddy, the best first pony a girl could ever have.*

## CHAPTER 1

*B*asil, assistant librarian at the Great Library of the Court of Knowledge, hurried back to the Library's center atrium, gripping the stack of papers he had copied. The Court of Sand had requested everything they had on thunderbirds, and it had taken longer than Basil would have liked to find and duplicate all the information.

The moss floor muffled the sounds of his boots. His dark green librarian coat flapped with his quick pace.

Winding shelves of books lined each of the walls and jutted into the room, creating a maze in each of the Library's many wings and rooms. Short trees grew from the mossy floor, and their broad leaves covered the skylights, providing a hazy, green daylight for the room while keeping the damaging direct sunlight from touching the precious books. Twigs grew from the bookshelves, leaves caressing the books protectively.

As Basil stepped around a bookshelf, the grand atrium came into view. Light beamed into the tall, many-stories-high room from the glass dome set in the ceiling. Underneath the dome grew a large, ancient tree with its roots spreading in all directions before disappearing deep into the moss.

Several of the master librarians sat at their desks built into the tall roots, directing the assistant librarians and taking questions from the fae who had come from far and wide for the information the Court of Knowledge provided.

A tall, male warrior from the Court of Sand stood next to one of the desks. His tunic left his arms bare, showing his muscles. A crooked, hawk's nose and flashing dark eyes turned in Basil's direction.

Basil resisted the urge to flinch away from the warrior's hard gaze as he hurried to the desk and held out the stack of paper to the master librarian behind the desk. "Master Librarian Domitius, here is the information you requested on thunderbirds."

Domitius snatched the papers from Basil, glaring. "Took you long enough."

Basil clenched his fists at his sides and swallowed back a retort. Of course it had taken a while. It wasn't like he had been sent for a single piece of information. He'd had to copy entire books on thunderbirds, not to mention track down historical battles against those monsters.

But he couldn't say any of that. Domitius wore the black coat of a master librarian while Basil still had the green coat of an assistant. That meant Basil had no choice but to answer to the master librarian, no matter how cantankerous.

At least, with the warrior from the Court of Sand standing there, Domitius wasn't being as insulting as he would otherwise. Instead, after that one jab, Domitius turned back to the warrior, handing over the papers with an ingratiating smile.

"Basil!" Another voice came from behind them.

Basil could have slumped in relief at the sound of Head

Librarian Marco's voice. Instead, he spun on his heels, only to stiffen and bow. "Your Majesties!"

Head Librarian Marco, wearing his black, gold-trimmed coat that designated him as the top librarian in the Library and the entire Court, strolled toward Basil. Marco wore his white hair long, and his beard reached all the way to his knees.

Next to him strolled King Theseus, ruler of the Court of Knowledge, with Queen Hippolyta of the Court of Sword-maidens at his side.

After years of trouble with both the Realm of Monsters and the other Courts—not everyone was happy with the results when they asked for knowledge from the Library, after all—King Theseus had turned to Queen Hippolyta of the Court of Swordmaidens. Her small island court of warrior women would provide protection for the otherwise un-warlike Court of Knowledge.

The pen might be mightier than the sword, but pens didn't do much against a cockatrice or a thunderbird or even the machinations of next-door courts like the Court of Revels run by the wild and unpredictable King Oberon and Queen Titania.

With his king and soon-to-be queen here in the Library, Basil hardly dared straighten from his bow. "How may I be of service?"

King Theseus glanced at Head Librarian Marco, raising an eyebrow.

Marco's mouth pressed in a tight line rather than its normal, good-natured grin. "Basil, we need you to research the marriage laws of our Court. Especially the punishments, obscure laws, that sort of thing. I assured the king that I would put my best librarian on the task."

Master Librarian Domitius might not appreciate how hard Basil worked, but at least Head Librarian Marco saw his worth. And if Marco trusted Basil with a task like this, then maybe he would finally give Basil the promotion to master librarian that he had been working toward for years.

Basil straightened. "I will see to it right away, sir, Your Majesties. Is there anything in particular I should look for?"

King Theseus and Queen Hippolyta exchanged a look before the king turned to Basil. "No."

By the tone, that was more a *No, I don't wish to explain,* rather than a *No, I have no preference*.

Perhaps King Theseus and Queen Hippolyta wanted to make sure nothing stood in the way of their marriage, since they were each rulers of their own Court. Such an alliance of Courts was rarely done, although Basil had thought King Theseus had followed all the necessary traditions. Not that the king and queen were too forthcoming with the details of how their binding came about.

These were desperate times. Thunderbirds attacking the Court of Sand. Krakens mauling the Court of Seas. A rise of monster attacks even here in the Court of Knowledge. Everywhere, the barrier between the Fae Realm and the Realm of Monsters was wearing thin.

Not that the king and queen had to explain their reasons to Basil. He was just a lowly assistant librarian. It was his job to follow orders, not question them.

"I will see to it and have the information to you as soon as possible." Basil bent in another bow. "Best wishes once again on your upcoming wedding, Your Majesties."

"Thank you." King Theseus glanced to Queen Hippolyta, a soft smile deepening the grooves around his mouth. "Four days."

"They will go by quickly." Queen Hippolyta shifted, turning to partially face King Theseus, causing the chain mail tunic she wore to clink. She held her head high, her golden hair wound in braids on her head as a crown, even as her light blue eyes shone with such love that Basil shifted, feeling almost awkward watching them. Her voice lowered, though it carried in the stillness of the Library. "After all, you have already bound my heart to yours."

Now Basil really wanted to be somewhere else. He backed away slowly, not wanting to draw attention to himself.

King Theseus took her hand, pressing a kiss to her knuckles. "Yes, when I captured your heart with my sword and the injuries I dealt you."

Queen Hippolyta's mouth quirked. "Keep telling yourself that. I seem to recall you were the one who spent time in my dungeon after you came begging for *my* sword and battle prowess. And you walked away from that encounter far more injured than I."

"I see I will have to prove my skills on Midsummer Night to win you all over again." King Theseus's tone was light, even if the glint in his eyes remained grim.

Basil shifted, glancing away. Midsummer Night was three days away. On that, the most magical night in this part of the Fae Realm, the barrier holding back the Realm of Monsters would be at its thinnest, endangering all of their Courts.

Thus the wedding was planned for the day after, hoping the love of the upcoming marriage would prevent the thin spots from growing too large. And so that, once the danger was over, they could all celebrate their survival.

If they survived.

Queen Hippolyta pulled her hand from the king's and sauntered toward the Library's exit. "You can try. But I am the one who already won you."

"I shall enjoy debating who stole whom in the years to come." King Theseus hurried to catch up with his soon-to-be bride.

"Ah, that's just it, Theseus-mine." Queen Hippolyta pushed open one of the two doors that led from the Great

Library to the Grand Hall that connected the library to the Court's castle. On the other side, two of Queen Hippolyta's swordmaidens stood at their posts, guarding the Library from monsters now that King Theseus and Queen Hippolyta would soon marry. The large door swung closed, cutting off the rest of Queen Hippolyta's reply.

Basil let out a breath, turned, and hurried away before anything else could happen. He had a task to complete.

He strode deeper into the Library, winding his way between the shelves. The small, scaled bookwyrms slithered on and around the bookshelves. As he passed one lounging on top of the books near shoulder height, he gave its head a pat, earning himself a raspy purr.

At the far end of one wing of the Library, Basil found the room dedicated to laws, both of their Court and of all the other Courts in the Fae Realm.

As he stepped inside, a strident voice he recognized echoed around the room.

"I would rather die than marry him!" Hermia yanked a book off the shelf with such force that a twig detached from the Library shelf and swatted her hand. She scowled at the twig before leafing through the book she held.

"That's exactly what your father is threatening!" Lysander's voice was only marginally less strident than Hermia's. Lysander's brown curls shone only slightly lighter than Basil's dark hair, though Lysander stood taller by several inches. Hermia's brown hair was lighter still, more mahogany than dark earth.

Both Lysander and Hermia wore green coats like Basil's, though their positions as assistant librarians were only temporary. They both came from noble families and were only working at the Great Library in preparation for their eventual positions in King Theseus' court.

The bookwyrms scattered, snorting puffs of hot air in their annoyance at all the noise.

"I don't care what my father wants! I love you, Lysander, not Demetrius." Hermia leaned closer to Lysander.

He cupped her face, then leaned down and kissed her.

Ugh. Basil was surrounded by people in love. It would be nauseating, if he wasn't so achingly jealous.

He cleared his throat.

Lysander and Hermia jumped apart, though Lysander still clutched Hermia's hand tightly as he faced Basil. "Bas! You have to help us."

Basil shook his head, starting to brush past them. "Sorry. I have a task for the king."

Lysander gripped Basil's arm, halting him. "But this is life or death! Hermia's father has invoked some arcane law to force her to marry Demetrius instead of me."

"What?" Basil blinked at the two of them. King Theseus's request hadn't been about his marriage to Queen Hippolyta at all. The king was trying to find a solution to keep the peace among his nobles.

Nor had Basil been chosen for this task because of his merits. It was solely because he was one of the few librarians without a tie to the nobles of the Court.

Basil's parents had been the librarians of the tiny village of Bog's End all the way at the edge of the Court of Knowledge. They had been killed the last time the barrier had worn this thin, leaving Basil alone. And, for King Theseus's purposes, free of sticky political or familial connections.

The romantic drama among the assistant librarians had been going on for several moons. It had been fine, at first. Lysander and Hermia had fallen in love with each other, and Demetrius and Helena, the other two noble fae assistant librarians working at the Great Library, had flirted.

But then Demetrius's father got it in his head that Helena was unsuitable and convinced Demetrius to change his affections from Helena to Hermia. At the same time, Hermia's father found out about her and Lysander, and, due to his ongoing feud with Lysander's father, had set out to break them up.

Helena took the change badly and became obsessive toward Demetrius while Demetrius turned stubborn in his determination to marry Hermia. What had been a group of friends turned into an angry, confusing mess.

And that mess had just taken a turn for the worse, if Hermia's father was now threatening to use some law to have her executed if she didn't marry Demetrius.

Lysander grimaced and placed his hand on his chest. "What does he have that I don't? My family is just as well placed as his."

"My father just doesn't like your father very much." Hermia gripped Lysander's arm, gazing at him with such a starry-eyed expression that Basil's stomach churned.

Though, he was not sure whether his churning stomach was from the overly sappy expression or jealousy. He had seen far too many of his fellow assistant librarians get that *look* and run off together over the years. While he still remained right where he was. Alone and trying to earn his master librarian's black coat.

At this point, the Great Library was all he had.

He schooled his features and faced Lysander and Hermia. "What did you want from me?"

Lysander gestured to the bookshelves lining the room. "Do you know of this law? Or a law that could override it? Please. Hermia's life is at stake!"

Basil rubbed at the back of his neck. "We will have to research to check, but from my understanding, any of the ancient rites of bonding override the others. Hermia's father could not arrange her marriage if you were already married."

"Of course!" Lysander turned to Hermia and gripped her shoulders. "We will run away together! Midsummer Night is three nights hence. If you can put your father off until then, we can join the Midsummer Revel in the Tanglewood. Surely if we are bound in that manner, your father will have no way to refute our binding."

The Revel. Basil had to suppress his grimace. On Midsummer Night, the Court of Revels, which shared the Tanglewood with the Court of Knowledge, hosted the Midsummer Revel, a time when young fae males and females ran around the forest until, eventually, they caught the one they were meant to be with. It was chaotic. Supposedly fun.

The Tanglewood was one of *those* enchanted forests. The ones where mysterious things happened. That which was tangled was made straight. Whatever was straight became tangled. Accepted truths became murky. Deceptions were torn away to reveal the truth. If Midsummer Night was the most magical time in the surrounding Courts, it was even more so in the Tanglewood.

Basil shook his head, suppressing his frown. "You're both going to be needed to protect the Library that night. Even the Revel and the Tanglewood will be dangerous."

"That's what Queen Hippolyta's swordmaidens are here for." Lysander waved back toward the main part of the Library. "Besides, we don't have a choice. As she knows my intentions, I cannot trick her into marriage. We are both from the same Court, so I can't steal her as my bride. We haven't managed to trigger a binding as fated mates, no matter what we have tried. Those are the only time-honored traditions that would hold enough weight to override her father's arranged marriage."

Lysander did have a point about that, much as Basil didn't like it. Even though he was annoyed with them, Lysander and Hermia—as well as Demetrius and Helena—were the

9

closest that Basil had to friends. "The Revel—and the Tangle-wood—is uncertain. You might not get the result you want."

"Of course we will. We are meant to be together. There might be some difficulties, but the course of true love never did run smooth." Lysander gazed down at Hermia, who stood only to his shoulder. He tucked a strand of her hair behind her tapered ear that was slightly tufted with fur.

Basil turned his back to them and walked to the shelves, though he didn't really see the titles. "You have a few days until Midsummer Night. I'll help you research if there is something else more solid than risking the Revel."

That was the task King Theseus had given him. As Lysander and Hermia were motivated, they might as well help.

They probably wouldn't find anything. The Fae Realm existed for such chaotic risk and mayhem, even here in the Court of Knowledge. Much as Basil didn't like it, especially when it came to the Revel.

"Don't worry about it, Bas. The Revel will be perfect!" Lysander grinned as he joined Basil at the bookshelf. "Actually, you should come too. Let loose a bit. You never know what might happen in the Tanglewood. Even you might stumble across the right female and find yourself bound before the night is over."

Basil's stomach churning sent bile all the way to his throat this time. None of his friends knew that he *had* joined the Revel. Once.

There had been this adorable assistant librarian with dark eyes and long dark hair and the wittiest conversation. He had thought she felt the same way about him. He had thought the Tanglewood would bind them.

He had even caught her that night, jubilant that the forest had indeed brought them together.

Instead, she had looked at him with a curl to her mouth,

those dark eyes flashing with disgust. "You? Why would I ever bind myself to you?" She'd yanked from his grip and run off into the forest then, leaving him alone.

Next time he'd seen her, she'd been bound to a fae noble in the Court of Revels, fully engaged in the riotous frivolity of that court.

"No. I'm never going to join the Revel." Basil had to spit the words between clenched teeth.

Hermia sighed and rolled her eyes. "Oh, come on, Bas. We all see how lonely you are. What other option do you have? You don't have parents to arrange a marriage for you. You aren't tricky enough to outsmart someone into a binding. About your only other option is to steal a bride. Or maybe let yourself be stolen."

The way she trailed off, looking away from him, said that she didn't think any fae would want to steal him, even if she didn't say it out loud.

Basil sighed and stared at the shelves in front of him. He wasn't boisterous like Lysander or noble in both bearing and features like Demetrius. He was just a mousy assistant librarian from a backwater like Bog's End.

Still, he so desperately wanted a mate that it ached in his chest. He wanted what his parents had. They had worked together in the village library. His childhood had been filled with laughter and smiles.

He had attained his dream of working at the Great Library. He spent his days with books and knowledge.

But it was far emptier than his life had been before his parents died.

"Maybe our friend Bas should go to the Human Realm to steal a bride. I've heard it's less dangerous to steal a human bride than snatching a bride from one of the other Courts." Lysander shrugged, also studying Basil. "Yes, I think a nice, quaint human would be just the thing for you. No fangs or claws or the wildness found in the Fae Courts."

"I don't think…" Basil found himself shaking his head, even as his mind was whirling.

Lysander thumped his shoulder. "Just think about it. It's either stay alone and miserable, join the Midsummer Revel, or steal a bride."

None of those sounded like great choices to him.

"Lysander!" Demetrius's shout rang through the Library, sending the bookwyrms hissing and slithering into hiding once again.

"We have to go." Lysander pushed away from the desk, and he and Hermia raced off.

Moments later, Demetrius, tall and blond-haired, strode around the corner. Blonde Helena dogged his heels, talking the entire time Demetrius walked, though he ignored her.

"Bas, have you seen Lysander? Or Hermia?" Demetrius crossed his arms, glancing around this corner of the Great Library.

"Demetrius, please!" Helena grabbed his arm. "It doesn't have to be this way."

Basil rubbed at his temples. Perhaps the Tanglewood was the only thing that could sort out this disaster.

No matter. Basil would do his best to stay out of it. He waved vaguely at the Library. "They were around a moment ago."

Jaw jutting, Demetrius stalked off, Helena still yapping behind him like a spaniel.

Basil groaned and let his forehead clunk onto the bookshelf. He needed at least one sensible person at his side. A nice, sensible fae female.

Was there such a thing?

"Basil!" The sharp tone yanked Basil's head up.

Master Librarian Domitius marched around one of the bookshelves. "Sleeping on the job, Basil?"

"No, sir." Basil straightened and reached for the nearest book, only to realize he'd pulled out a book on the laws of the Swamp Court. He quickly shoved it back onto the shelf.

"Don't keep the king waiting." The master librarian's lip curled as he glanced from Basil to the shelves. "You are trying my patience with your repeated laziness. But I guess that's what comes from hiring a librarian from a place like Bog's End."

"I won't let it happen again." Basil gritted his teeth. He'd done nothing wrong. Besides, he was the only one actually working. Helena, Demetrius, Hermia, and Lysander were all too wrapped up in their romantic drama to do their jobs.

But Master Librarian Domitius never blamed them. They were noble fae. They could do no wrong, no matter how little work they accomplished.

"See that it doesn't. You can be replaced, you know. There are plenty of librarians in the Court who would cut off an arm for your position." Master Librarian Domitius swept off, his black coat sweeping behind him.

Basil faced the shelves and got to work. He would find the requested information, vague as his instructions were, even if he had to stay up all night to do it. This job at the Great Library was all he had left.

No family. No friends. No mate.

He really was one of the most miserable fae in the entire Court of Knowledge.

Perhaps he was just desperate enough to join the Revel again. Or, maybe, steal a human bride.

$\mathcal{M}$eg hunched under the scorching sun, chopping the weeds that struggled to grow from the dead-dry ground. Sweat dripped down her back underneath the brown rag of a dress she wore.

She wasn't sure why she bothered. The crops languished even more than the weeds in this drought.

Next to her, Viola and Beatrice, her two youngest sisters, knelt on the ground, picking out the weeds that were too close to the frail corn sprouts for Meg to risk chopping with the hoe.

Across the farm field, Brigid, the younger sister closest in age to Meg, hauled a bucket of water from the creek, which was down to a mere trickle that would die completely if they didn't get rain soon. Behind her, Meg's only brother Sebastian staggered back to the creek with his empty bucket after he had carefully trickled water onto a row of corn.

Their farm fields spread along the edge of the forest, a small plot of land carved from the forest's grasp sometime in the generations long past and long forgotten. Their ramshackle hovel stood at the far end of their land, its grayed boards peeling and leaving large gaps that let in the hot, dusty winds.

It would let in the rain, too, if they ever got rain.

"Meg!" Brigid waved, then pointed.

When Meg looked in that direction, her stomach sank. Five riders on large, well-fed horses galloped down the road from the nearest village. A well-muscled, blond-haired man rode in the lead.

"Girls, get inside." Meg reached down and nudged first Beatrice, then Viola.

They glanced up, their eyes widening, before they jumped to their feet and raced toward the hut.

Brigid and Sebastian joined Meg, standing on either side of her.

The sun beat down, scorching Meg's face and burning hot against the back of her neck. She glanced to each of them. "You two should go inside as well."

Brigid crossed her arms. "Not a chance. I'm not leaving you out here alone with that slug."

"I won't let him take you away." Sebastian clenched his fists, his face hard. At fourteen, he was far too young to defend his sisters against five grown men, but he seemed determined to try if it came to that.

If Cullen was here for Meg, there was nothing anyone could do.

She had run out of time to send Brigid and Sebastian to the hovel. They would have to face Cullen together.

They hurried across the field as quickly as possible, but Cullen still directed his horse and his men off the road, heedlessly trampling the corn sprouts. He reined his light brown horse to a stop in front of Meg, the animal tossing its head and rolling its eyes at the rough hand on the reins. His cronies halted their horses behind him, their faces hard.

If Meg had any power, she would save that horse from him. But she couldn't even save herself.

Cullen didn't even bother dismounting. He leaned on the saddle's high pommel, staring down at Meg with cold, blue eyes. His blond hair was trimmed meticulously short, down to the short beard that covered his chin.

Meg met his gaze, her chin held high. She didn't dare back down. "What do you want, Cullen? Our next payment isn't due until next week."

"I am just checking on my…investment." Cullen should have glanced at the fields. Those struggling corn seedlings were what his money had funded.

But he swept his cool gaze over Meg. Not leering. Not coveting her for himself. No, Cullen was taking stock of her, calculating how much he could get for her indenture.

For Cullen, this drought had been an opportunity. When farms faltered, he gave them loans with impossibly high interest. When they failed, he bought them outright. And when nothing more of worth could be drained from the earth, he sold the only commodity this land had left. Its people.

Sure, slavery was illegal. But that didn't stop those like Cullen from prettying it up with a name like indentured servitude. It still amounted to the same thing, when people were sold for indentures so high and worked with pay so low that they could never earn their way free, even if that possibility was dangled in front of them to torture them with hope.

For Meg, cursed with her mother's golden-blonde hair and beautiful face, she knew exactly what work her indenture would involve.

Cullen's mouth gave a little twist, and he straightened. "Until next week. Don't work yourself too hard, Margaret. I would hate to have my investment damaged before I come to claim it."

With a sharp kick of his heels, he sent his horse into a trot. His band of henchmen followed, a silent wall of muscle that Meg had no hope of fighting or outrunning.

Meg finally forced her muscles to move when Cullen and his men were nothing but a cloud of dust on the horizon.

"I won't let him take you." Sebastian turned serious blue eyes to Meg. "You can't leave. Not like Pa."

Meg rested a hand on her brother's shoulder. He was shorter than her, still a child with growing to do. Her throat choked too much for her to respond to him.

Two years ago, their father had sacrificed himself to Cullen and had been sold into an indenture, buying the rest of them time.

Nine months after he had been taken away, word had come through the grapevine of scattered families that he had died.

Their mother, already weak thanks to the drought, had died only three months after that.

If Cullen had his way, Meg would be next. Her whole family would be sold, one by one, until none of them would be left. A bleak, unthinkable future.

What could Meg do to stop it? She was powerless. Penniless. Helpless.

Escape. That was Meg's only option. She'd have to run.

What about her brother? Her sisters? She couldn't abandon them to Cullen's clutches.

She couldn't leave them.

If she stayed, she would be forced to leave them anyway.

Perhaps she could go out into the world and find some way to earn money. She could find a better life for them.

Meg glanced around at the withering fields, the burning sun high overhead. Hope was such a foolish thing. She didn't have any money to even make it to the next town, much less get far enough away to find a place untouched by the drought. Nor did she have a way to earn that needed money. No one needed farmhands right now. No one had extra money to hire a seamstress or a cook.

Her only option would be to sell herself into the same future that Cullen planned for her. It would make no difference, in the end.

Her gaze snagged on the forest. It was the only thing that retained any semblance of green, though only a few dry leaves still filled the canopy.

It gave her an idea. A risky idea.

But she was desperate enough that she might just try it. After all, she didn't have anything left to lose.

THAT EVENING, Meg gathered her siblings around the old, scarred table in the kitchen. From ten-year-old Beatrice with wide, scared eyes to thirteen-year-old Viola standing next to Sebastian. Barely a year apart, the two of them had grown up nearly as twins. Next to them, sixteen-year-old Brigid crossed her arms, as if already prepared to argue with whatever Meg had to say.

Not that Meg could blame her sister. This plan was crazy. Honestly, she was already arguing with herself over it. But, at nineteen, she was the adult in this family. The decision was up to her.

Meg drew in a deep breath, facing them. "I am going to run away to the forest tonight."

For a moment, all her siblings just stared at her. Then, Beatrice's eyebrows scrunched. "Mama said never to go into the forest at night because the faeries would take us."

"Yes, exactly." Meg gripped the table to hide her shaking

hands. "The faeries have gold and jewels. If I get myself snatched by a faerie lord, he can afford to pay off Cullen."

"Meg, no. You can't be serious." Brigid shook her head. "You know the stories. You know what the fae will want from you."

"It isn't any worse than what I'm facing if I let Cullen sell me into an indenture. At least with the fae, I'll have a chance to bargain." Meg swallowed, working to keep her voice steady. She knew how risky this was. How slim the chance that this future would be any better than the one she left behind.

But hope was a tricky thing. It was hard to let it go, hard not to pursue it, even when the odds of success were so small.

Meg held Brigid's gaze. "You know I have no choice. This is our only chance to save our family. If we can pay off Cullen, then the rest of you can be saved from indenture."

"And if Cullen wonders where we got gold? If he pressures us to give him more? Threatens us to tell him our source?" Brigid kept glaring back.

"Then I'll have a fae lord husband to protect everyone." Surely she could bargain for that much.

"Meg…" Sebastian stepped forward, jaw hard. "I can protect us."

"I know. And I am depending on you to protect everyone until I can return with the gold." Meg flicked her gaze from Brigid to Sebastian and back. "Use our savings to pay off Cullen. That will buy you time, and you won't need as much to buy food with me gone. I'll be back as soon as I can."

When Sebastian nodded, Meg faced Brigid once again, sharing a look with what she couldn't say out loud in front of the younger siblings. "Cullen most likely won't come for you right away. But if he does, then you run, got it? If I'm not back within a year, then you all run. You get as far away from here as possible."

Brigid held Meg's gaze and gave a solemn nod. If Meg's family ran, then there was little chance Meg would ever see them again. She would have no way of finding them, unless they also ran to the forest and were snatched by fae. Even then, they would likely be split apart forever.

Still, they would have a better chance by running than staying here, if it came to that.

They had time. At sixteen, Brigid had yet to fully come into her adult beauty. Cullen would wait to sell her until he knew he could get top dollar for her indenture. Same with Sebastian and the younger girls.

But if the drought ended, Cullen would jump to sell them regardless of what he could get out of them before he lost his chance.

It was a risk to leave them all behind, but Meg didn't dare take them with her now. They would give the fae who snatched her too much power over her. Nor did she want her siblings to see what she had to do to bargain for their safety. Whatever happened, Meg had to do it alone.

Meg had nothing to pack. Her sisters would need her spare dress and worn shoes more than she would. Brigid tried to press a shriveled, dried apple and a scrap of bread into Meg's hands, but Meg refused. If the stories weren't true and a fae didn't snatch her for simply stepping into that forest at night, then it wouldn't matter if she had food with her or not. She would be dead already.

She hugged each of her siblings, pressing a kiss to the foreheads of each of the younger girls as she tried to ignore the tears streaking their cheeks and the way their arms held her so very tightly.

It took all of her strength to let them go and walk to the door. She had to heave upward on the door as she swung it out. She refused to pause as she shoved the sagging door shut on her last glimpse of her family.

She drew in a deep breath of the crisp night air, and it tasted like freedom and hope. A sliver of moon bathed the night in a dark silver. The hard-packed earth felt cool and dusty beneath her bare feet as she marched across her family's field, carefully stepping over each row of corn.

As she walked into the forest, a cold breeze swirled around her, shivering against the dried sweat beneath her thin dress.

It had sounded so easy, back there in her family's hut. But now, alone in the night, each shadow prickled the hair on the back of Meg's neck.

She was probably more likely to be eaten by a wolf than get snatched by a mythical fae, but, honestly, what other choice did she have? Getting eaten would be a miserable death, but it would still be faster than the miserable death that Cullen had planned for her.

She could barely see as she pushed her way through the waist-high ferns and the saplings struggling upward underneath the large, tangled trees rising into the sky. Moonlight attempted to pierce the leaves spreading overhead.

The layer of last fall's leaves were damp and squishy beneath Meg's feet, even after the drought, with the occasional fallen branch or stone poking at her toes. Even though it was nearly midsummer, a chill filled the forest, and Meg hugged her arms around her waist and shivered in her thin, ragged dress.

Perhaps she wouldn't get eaten by wolves. She could just freeze to death. Or die of thirst and starvation wandering lost in this forest.

Still, she trudged onward if for nothing else but the sheer stubbornness of it. If she perished, it would be after a good try at surviving.

Ahead, a section of the forest glowed brighter, and Meg stumbled her way toward it. She pushed through a thicker stand of undergrowth and popped into a small, circular clearing.

This was a too-perfect circle. The forest should have encroached, yet this circle remained clear of so much as a sapling or fern. Instead, the ground was covered with a moss that felt soft and almost warm beneath Meg's bare feet. As she drew in a deep breath, the air felt thicker. Moonlight shimmered, and a full moon hung overhead instead of the crescent that had lit Meg's way earlier.

Meg didn't know anything about fae and magic, but this place reeked of *something* not of her world of drought and dying farm fields.

If she was going to get herself snatched by the fae, this would be the place.

Meg plopped down on the moss. This wasn't a great plan. Downright foolhardy, come to think of it.

But she had no good options.

She could venture into a town and hope she wasn't mugged or killed or hurt or apprehended by Cullen.

Or she could pin her hopes on a mythical fae warrior coming to steal her away and bargain with him for a halfway decent life for herself and her siblings.

She settled into a more comfortable position on the moss. Hopefully the magic pressing down on this clearing would keep the wolves at bay while she waited for a fae to show up and steal her away.

## CHAPTER 3

*A*fter a long day at the library, Basil tottered his way through the Anywhere Door that connected the Great Library to his small cottage in the village. It was tempting just to lie down on the moss carpet and fall asleep right there in the middle of his kitchen.

A crunching came from the other side of a double door set into the wall on one side of the kitchen. After a rustling and clomping, Basil's talking pony companion Buddy stuck his head over the bottom half of the door, blinking and still chewing on a mouthful of sweet grass and clover. He was a stocky pony with glossy brown fur and a thick brown-black mane. White spots on the end of his nose and the middle of his forehead were his only markings.

Buddy spoke around his mouthful. "You're late. Again."

"It was a rough day." Basil stumbled across the tiny cottage and crawled into the nook in the wall filled with a moss mattress and piled with blankets. He tugged off his boots and his coat, dropping them on the floor.

"The Foolish Four were at it again, were they?" Buddy snorted and shook his head, sending his thick forelock swinging over his deep brown eyes. "How they are considered a part of the Court of Knowledge, I will never know. Though, it is the Court of Knowledge, and even knowledge can be foolish if not applied correctly."

"And I suppose you ponies are the true founts of wisdom?" Basil lay down, his hands behind his head. Only with Buddy could he relax enough to be himself.

"Of course. Only we equines possess true sense. You fae are all too flighty and wild, though you are one of the more sensible of the lot."

"Thanks, I think." Basil heaved a sigh, staring at the ceiling. "Lysander and Hermia plan to abandon the Library on Midsummer Night to join the Revel, which means Demetrius and Helena will follow them. Of all years to leave the Library shorthanded on Midsummer Night, this is a bad one."

"I would say that maybe it won't be as bad as you fear, considering you'll have the help of Queen Hippolyta's swordmaidens this year, but…" Buddy bared his teeth in the horse version of a grimace. "I met a friend of mine from the Court of Revels today. The Deplorable Duo are at each other's throats again, and it looks like it will only get worse before it gets better."

Basil scrubbed both hands over his face, resisting the urge to groan. He wasn't sure if the groan was because King Oberon and Queen Titania of the Court of Revels were fighting or because of Buddy's irreverent nickname for them.

Marital strife between a king and queen was bad even during a normal time of the year. It threw whole Courts into chaos and often dragged other, surrounding Courts into the fray. Not to mention things like anger and hatred wore holes in the barrier to the Realm of Monsters, creating more attacks.

But on Midsummer Night when the magic of this Realm was so strong, everything would be magnified. More anger, more strife, would mean an abundance of monster attacks that even the swordmaidens might have trouble fending off.

Basil flopped one arm over his eyes. "The next few days are not going to be pleasant."

"Wild and foolish, I tell you." Buddy gave a loud snort that probably spewed horse mucus onto the floor. "Only humans manage to be more foolish, though some aren't so bad."

"Today, Lysander suggested I steal a human bride. Can you believe it?" Basil shook his head, staring at the ceiling. Why was he struggling to laugh the thought away? He should not find it intriguing.

"Actually, it isn't a bad idea." Buddy bobbed his head. "Get yourself a nice girl. Someone who can help you in the Great Library and provide a buffer from the antics of the Foolish Four. Besides, stealing a bride would raise your status, you know. Most fae take the easy route of joining the Revel or arranging a marriage nowadays. Your fellow librarians will be impressed if you steal a bride."

Sure, but that involved danger and venturing into the Human Realm. Basil might be willing to fight to defend the Library and its precious store of books, but he wasn't going to borrow trouble.

"Until you find a mate of your own, I'm not going to listen to any of your advice." Basil rolled over to put his back to Buddy. "Now stop talking and let me sleep."

The half door creaked, then Buddy's hooves thudded softly on the moss floor.

A moment later, Buddy's large, blunt teeth clamped around Basil's arm.

Basil gave a cry as Buddy yanked him from the nook. He landed on the floor, his arm aching. "What did you do that for?"

"You're going to go steal a bride. Tonight." Buddy pressed

his muzzle close to Basil, blowing hot breath smelling of grass in his face.

"What? You can't be serious. I have work tomorrow. I need my sleep." The last thing Basil wanted to do was go out into the night, ride Buddy to the edge of the Tanglewood where a circle of stones marked a permanent thin spot that connected to the Human Realm, and then stumble into an unknown realm searching for some random human girl to snatch.

Basil tried to crawl back into bed, but Buddy nipped the back of his trousers.

With a huff, Basil plopped onto the floor, rubbing at his rear end. "You can be such a mule sometimes."

"Don't insult my parentage." Buddy bared his teeth. They might have been blunt, but they were large and could bite one of Basil's fingers off like a carrot if Buddy chose.

Not that Basil was truly worried that his pony companion would turn on him like that, but it still sent a skittering through his stomach.

"Now listen up, Bas." Buddy glared down at him, as much as a pony with wild hair and soft brown eyes could glare. "You have been a mild-mannered librarian from the tiny hamlet of Bog's End for too long. If you don't do something soon, your fellow librarians will always stomp all over you. It is time to take a stand like you were born with four legs instead of two useless ones and prove that there is more to you than they think. I would have wandered off to find a different fae companion long ago if I didn't believe there was more to you than met the eye."

"And you think stealing a bride is going to do that?" Basil stopped rubbing his rear end to rub at his temples instead. His eyes hurt with how much he needed sleep.

"I'm not saying you should try to steal a bride from the Court of Swordmaidens like King Theseus. A warrior bride would kill you." Buddy snorted again, spraying Basil's face with horse snot. "A human would be a lot safer in the long run. But the dangers of the Human Realm would still be enough to prove your bravery. With the magic so high right now, you'll never have an easier time getting to the Human Realm than now, unless you go on Midsummer Night when the barrier will be so thin even a human might be able to wander into our realm by mistake."

Basil's chest tightened. While humans themselves were a lot weaker and frailer than even a fae like him, their realm held dangers that made most fae avoid it whenever possible. Their iron burned and weakened. The very realm itself put limitations and rules on fae—like not being able to lie—that weren't present in the Fae Realm. It was dangerous just to step foot in the Human Realm.

Basil squeezed his eyes shut, remembering the way Master Librarian Domitius felt free to blame Basil for everything that went wrong in the Library. Lysander and Demetrius called themselves his friends, yet they never bothered to treat him with respect. Helena and Hermia ignored him unless they wanted something from him.

And that fellow assistant librarian who had made no secret that he was the last person she wanted to catch her during the Midsummer Revel.

Fine. He was going to show them all that there was more to this assistant librarian.

"All right, Buddy. Let's go to the Human Realm."

## CHAPTER 4

*S*omeone was shaking Meg's shoulder.

She had overslept. Her siblings needed her in the fields. Or Cullen had arrived.

Meg bolted upright. "I'm up. I'm…"

It wasn't morning. The moonlit clearing still surrounded her, the air so heavy with a glittering, floral taste that she could barely breathe. Soft moss cushioned her instead of the hard, straw pallet she slept on at home.

A stranger knelt in front of her. His brown-black hair framed his face, long enough to fall across his forehead. The points of his tapered ears were visible while his face was thinner, more angular than a human's. Even in the moonlight, his skin appeared a darker bronze than hers. Deep brown eyes peered at her beneath dark, expressive eyebrows.

He was definitely a fae. And he was certainly handsome.

More than that, he was nicely dressed in what looked like dark gray trousers and a shirt that was either light gray or white beneath a dark green coat that looked like something a noble would wear. He was slim but not thin in a way that would suggest he lacked for food. Not the same way she was, with her bones jutting out against her skin.

Behind him, a brown pony stuck its head over the fae's shoulder, snuffling at her face before blowing a gust of hot breath. Besides the shaggy mane and tail, the pony's coat gleamed in the moonlight, its barrel-shaped stomach filled out in a way she had only seen on Cullen's horses.

"Are you a faerie lord?" Meg bit her lip. Of course he was a lord. He had a horse, owned sturdy clothes, and both he and his pony were well fed. He had to be rich enough that he could care for her better than anything she could expect here. "Whatever you are, I guess you'll do. You aren't the violent type, are you?"

The fae rocked back on his heels. Then he said something she couldn't understand.

Great. She hadn't counted on a language barrier. That would make things interesting.

Oh, well. She wasn't out here hoping for romance or some nonsense like that. All she wanted was a full belly, a nice dress, and enough gold to buy her family's freedom from Cullen. She didn't need this fae to actually talk to her for that.

"Well, are you going to snatch me or not? I'm not sure how this whole stealing thing works." Meg held out her hand toward the fae.

He glanced over his shoulder at his pony. The pony bobbed its head, then bumped the fae toward her with its nose.

The fae said something else in his lilting language, then took her hand and pulled her to her feet. She didn't resist as he led her to the pony, then lifted her onto its back, his hands strong around her waist.

Then he sprang onto the pony behind her.

Her goose was plucked, right enough. No turning back

29

now. She'd gotten herself snatched by a fae. Now she could only hope it was a better future than the one she'd run from.

WHEN HE'D SET out to steal a human bride, Basil hadn't expected to find one waiting for him in the faerie circle. To be honest, he'd half-expected that he would ride through the thin spot to the Human Realm, search the forest for a couple of hours to satisfy Buddy, then go home without finding any human girl to steal away.

But there she had been. Sleeping on the moss with her blonde hair a mess around her, dirty feet and face, and a ragged dress draped over her tiny frame.

Were all humans this bony and emaciated? She was so tiny in his arms as Buddy took them back through the thin spot, arriving on the other side at the edge of the Tanglewood.

The human girl in his arms gasped, her mouth falling open as she stared around at the broad trunks reaching for the sky with twisting branches draped in thick strands of moss and vines. Glowing flowers grew from some of the vines, shining gold and silver.

Basil stared down at the top of her head. This close to her, she smelled terrible. Did all humans reek like this?

What had he been thinking to let Buddy talk him into this? Why had he thought it a good idea to steal a human girl?

He should put her back. Perhaps if he did it quickly enough, the magical bindings wouldn't have a chance to set in.

"Rustling raccoons, what is this place?" The girl gaped upward at the full, blue moon high above.

Basil let out a long, deflating breath. Too late. They had

already been magically bound. He could still extricate himself, but it would be a lot more complicated. Far easier—and less dangerous—to finish the binding and be done with it.

He reached to set a hand on her shoulder but stopped short. This was awkward. He'd thought finding a girl at the Revel would be bad, but this was worse. Much worse. "This is, uh, the Fae Realm."

"Right, of cour—" The girl started, then swung around so quickly that she would have fallen from Buddy's back if Basil hadn't gripped her around the waist. "You can understand me? And I can understand you? But I couldn't before."

Buddy snorted and shook his shaggy mane. "No, you couldn't. But you went willingly when he stole you away, so that started the binding."

The girl shrieked and lurched so violently that Basil barely caught her before she could slide from Buddy's back. She curled into Basil, scrabbling at him as if trying to get away from the pony whose back she was sitting on. "Your pony talks!"

Buddy glanced at the two of them, focusing on the girl. "I am not *his* pony. If anything, he is *my* fae. I am Sir Buddy the Magnificent, of the estimable line of talking equine companions."

If anything, the girl's mouth gaped open even more. "Talking equine companion?"

"He means that we have an agreement." Basil wasn't sure if he should try to pry the girl's clinging grip off him or let her be. "He provides transportation and companionship—"

"And wise advice. Don't forget the wise advice," Buddy added.

Basil wasn't sure how wise he'd call Buddy's advice, especially at the moment. But he wasn't going to argue in front of

31

the human girl. "And I provide him with shelter, all the clover he can eat, and the protection of my Court."

"Ah, I see." The girl relaxed, pushing away from Basil as if realizing how twined she'd been around him. She stared down at her hands, fidgeting. "And a stolen human wife? What do you provide her?"

His face and neck burned. "I, uh…" He swallowed and tried to gather his fizzling thoughts. He really should have thought this plan through first before he'd let Buddy talk him into it. Come to think of it, there hadn't been much of a plan besides go to the Human Realm, snatch a girl, and bring her back. He hadn't thought about what would happen after-wards. "Whatever you want. Within reason, of course. I'm not a prince or anything. But…well, I guess whatever normal stuff a mate would give his wife in your world."

There was something odd about the way she had asked that question, but Basil wasn't sure what it was.

In front of him, her shoulders remained tense. "So what is this binding? And why does it mean I can now understand you?"

Basil held out his hand, palm up. "Take my hand."

She raised her eyebrows but rested her hand on top of his. A soft, yellow glow surrounded their fingers. Eyes widening, she snatched her hand back. "What is that?"

"The binding. It means we are magically bound together." Basil shrugged as the glow faded now that their hands were no longer touching.

"Like…we're married now?" The girl's nose wrinkled as she rubbed her palm, as if she couldn't believe it had been glowing a moment ago.

"No, not yet. We still need to complete the marriage bind-ing. And the binding will stop glowing once we do." Basil stared at the moon in the sky above them for a moment, trying to think of how to explain this. "This binding is like a betrothal, I guess you'd call it in your world. But it is stronger than that. Once two people are bound, it is rather difficult to undo the binding."

Buddy shifted beneath them, then swung his head around. "Basil, you're giving the poor girl a lecture."

Basil winced. He had a tendency to spout more information than a person wanted to know. He shut his mouth before he explained more about the other bindings, like the binding of a person to a Court or the binding of a prisoner or how the marriage binding was the strongest of all and could break or change the others. Not to mention all the ways a marriage binding could be triggered. It was all rather complicated.

"Now, if you don't mind, the two of you are rather heavy. I'm going to get moving." Without waiting for a reply, Buddy started walking once again, headed toward the village.

The girl faced forward and dug her fingers into Buddy's mane, her head bent. "Where are we going? And what happens now?"

Basil tugged at his collar, the coat and shirt suddenly too hot and constricting. He was going to burn up from embarrassment before the night was over. He seriously underestimated how awkward stealing a bride was going to be. Perhaps the Revel would have been easier after all.

But at this point, he was partially bound to this human already. As an assistant librarian, he knew all the stories of what happened when a binding was left undone. Thankfully, they had Buddy to act as a witness, so he didn't have to get anyone else involved.

"We are going to perform the marriage ceremony, then we go home." Basil fished in an inner pocket of his librarian coat and located bookbinding thread. "Hold out your hand."

Buddy gave a huff. "This would probably be easier if you got down."

"But then we'd have to climb right back up again." Basil rolled his eyes. "We can do the ceremony on our way."

"Fine. If that's how you want it. I was just thinking you should make this a romantic moment and all that." Ponies couldn't raise their eyebrows, but Buddy's expression suggested that he would if he could. "Besides, I wouldn't mind the rest. I'm a pony, not a horse. I'm not really big enough to carry two people for long distances."

"You'll be fine for the short stroll to the village." Basil tentatively touched the girl's shoulder. "What would you prefer?"

She jumped, leaning forward to put more space between them. "Let's just keep going and get this over with."

Did that mean she was not the type to want romance? Or was it just too awkward for her as well? Was she eager to see his home? Getting a mate was a whole lot more complicated than he had expected.

With a shaky breath, the girl swiveled as much as she could and held out her right hand. "So how does this work? Do I have to slash my palm, seal our marriage in blood, or something like that?"

"Of course not. What kind of barbarians do you humans think we fae are?"

"You did just steal me away in the middle of the night."

Point taken.

"All we're going to do is tie the knot." Tucking the middle of the string against his palm, Basil clasped her hand, her fingers tiny and warm in his grasp. The glow surrounded their hands again. He wound one half of the string around their clasped hands and his wrist. "With this binding, I pledge myself to you."

After a moment, the girl fumbled with the other half of the string and copied his movements to wrap the string around their hands and her wrist. She cleared her throat, flicking a glance at him before staring back down at their hands. "With this binding, I pledge myself to you."

The growing shiver of magic closed around them with such pressure Basil had to work to swallow. The brightness of their glowing, clasped hands made him squint. "Now we tie the ends together to complete the binding."

It was awkward, trying to work with the girl to tie the two ends of the string together, especially since they were riding Buddy. But, after several moments, they managed a sloppy knot.

The gathering magic settled on them, then flared along the knotted string. With a flash, the string unwound from them, divided itself into two pieces, and settled on each of their wrists, melding into itself into their skin as a thin, gold line.

That was that. The binding was complete. He had a human wife.

And he didn't even know her name.

"So that's it?" The girl withdrew her hand and rubbed the gold line around her wrist, frowning.

"Yes. We are bound to each other as mates. The magical binding will protect you from faerie fruit or trickery that could have ensnared you had you entered our realm unbound to anyone. It also gives me some protection from things that can trap the fae in your realm." Basil cleared his throat, glancing past her shoulder to the road ahead. The palace and library were closer now, along with his cottage in the library's shadow. "My name is Basil, by the way."

"Mar—" The girl cut herself off, staring forward instead of craning her neck to look at Basil. When she spoke, it was with an extra forcefulness. "Meg. My name is Meg."

Meg. It was a nice name. Short and cute and somehow perfectly suited to the button-nosed girl sitting on Buddy in front of him.

Basil gestured toward the twin sets of spires rising before them, connected by the square, grand hall. "The castle on the left is where King Theseus rules our court, the Court of Knowledge. On the right is the Great Library. That's where I work. I'm an assistant librarian."

He couldn't help the warm note of pride in his voice as he took in the Library. The white stones of both castle and library gleamed in the moonlight, a shining beacon containing all the wisdom and knowledge found in the Fae Realm and even much of the knowledge gleaned from the Human Realm.

"Huh." The sound was decidedly less impressed than he had been expecting.

They entered the village that clustered along the outer walls of the library and castle. Meandering streets wound between the cottages and shops. Laughter, talking, and music filled the streets lit with faerie lights. Fae like himself bustled about or gathered in groups talking or playing games. Pixies flitted above their heads while brownies lurked in the shadows.

The night was as busy as the day in the Fae Realm, even in the Court of Knowledge. Basil had heard that the Court of Revels was even more chaotic in its revelries during the night, but he had never ventured there in the evening hours, nor did he wish to do so.

Meg gawked at everything they passed, and Basil explained what he could. There were some things even he couldn't exactly explain. This was the Fae Realm, after all.

Finally, they arrived at his cottage, tucked into a quiet alley not far from the outer wall of the Library. As Buddy halted, Basil slid to the ground. Before he could help Meg, she hopped off, landing lightly. Her gaze swept over the cottage, from the thatched roof to the square stone walls. A lean-to rested against one side for Buddy.

Her mouth tipped down into something almost like a frown.

Basil's stomach knotted. His cottage wasn't much to look at from the outside, especially not compared to the grandeur of the castle or the Great Library looming above them. Or even the larger homes across the river where the courtiers lived.

But it wasn't a hovel by any means. It was a respectable home, and it had plenty of secrets hidden on the inside that weren't visible from the outside.

Instead of lifting the latch, Basil rested his hand on the door. "Here. Place your hand next to mine. The magic in my home will sense that you now belong here and will rearrange the inside for you."

Meg's forehead scrunched, but she placed her fingers next to his on the door.

The whole cottage shivered, then a burst of glittering light burped from the house, spilling around the door and out each of the windows, even the doorway of Buddy's stall.

Buddy shook his mane, then trotted toward his door. "You better not have messed with my stall."

"Walloping weasels, this place is weird." Meg blinked at the doorway, this time sounding more impressed.

Basil lifted the latch and pushed the door open, not sure what to expect. The cottage changed to accommodate whatever was required. It had added Buddy's lean-to after Buddy became Basil's talking equine companion. Who knew what would happen when he gained a stolen human bride?

The door swung open, and the faerie lights inside automatically winked to life, bobbing in gleaming spheres at the ceiling.

Basil gestured. "After you."

Meg glanced at him, as if suspecting this was some kind of trap. After a moment, she shrugged and stepped inside.

## CHAPTER 5

*M*eg wiggled her toes on the soft moss carpeting the floor of Basil's house. No, not just Basil's house, but her new home. A strange thought.

She rubbed at her temples as she turned in a circle, taking in the room. To her right, a double door was set into the wall, the upper door latched open against the wall. Buddy already stuck his head over the lower door. He gave her a large, buck-toothed smile.

Talking ponies. That would take some getting used to.

Directly in front of her, a small set of cupboards had been grown out of twisting branches. Not a single side or opening was straight, and it was enough to set her head to spinning. A small table with two chairs stood in the center of the room in front of the kitchen cupboards.

Next to the kitchen, a door fashioned of twisting branches that somehow fit so tightly together that there were no gaps was set into the wall.

Along the wall to her right two cushioned chairs cozied up to a fireplace.

It was a nice house. Far more snug and sturdy than the hut she had left behind.

Still, it wasn't the lordly castle she had been envisioning when she ran away. Did Basil have enough riches to pay off Cullen?

What if she had made a mistake, in running off with the first fae that came to snatch her? What would she do if Basil wasn't rich enough to help? Assistant librarian didn't exactly sound like a high-paying job.

"This is interesting." Basil strode into the cottage behind her, closing the door. When she glanced at him, he gestured at the fireplace and chairs. "That wasn't there before. My sleeping nook used to be against that wall."

Her stomach gave a flip, and she hugged her arms tightly over her middle. Was it a good sign or a bad sign that his sleeping nook disappeared? She glanced around again. Where were they going to sleep? Was the bedroom through the door on the far side of the room? Her head hurt trying to think about a cottage rearranging itself.

"I guess the bedrooms must have been added to the Anywhere Door." Basil strolled around her, lurching to avoid touching her in the small space in the center of the cottage. He gripped the latch of the door across the room from where she stood. "The Anywhere Door leads to wherever you need it to, as long as there is another Anywhere Door in that place. It mostly opens other rooms in the house or it takes me to the Library."

"It leads me to the best patch of grass and clover in all of the Fae Realm." Buddy breathed out a long sigh through his large nostrils.

"I…see." She didn't. What kind of door didn't always lead to the same place every time? That made no sense whatsoever.

Basil swung the door open, then peered around the door

frame. Inside, a nook was carved into the far wall, piled with rumpled blankets. A few items of clothing were scattered around on the floor or hung inside an open wardrobe. Basil hastily shut the door. "Um, well, that's my room. Let's try this again."

When he opened the door again, the revealed room was almost identical to the first, but the blankets in the nook were pristine and no clothing was scattered about. A few flowers grew out of the walls and from the moss carpeting the floor.

Basil's shoulders relaxed, and a tight smile flashed across his face. "This must be your room."

Meg could have hugged the house. Her own room. That was a relief. She might have been willing to be snatched and marry a strange fae, but she had been dreading just jumping into the whole marriage thing.

Her own room. Whatever else Basil was like, this cottage and that room were already an improvement from what she would have had if she had stayed in her own realm.

Too bad it might not be enough to save the rest of her family.

Basil closed the door, stepped back, then waved at it. "Why don't you try it out? It's getting late, and I'm sure you'll want some rest."

She had been too keyed up after leaving her family, stumbling through the forest, getting snatched by this fae, and marrying him on the spot to even feel her exhaustion. Plus, she had slept for a while in that faerie clearing.

But, now that he mentioned it, her shoulders ached from all the tension, and her eyes felt gritty.

The moss was spongy beneath her feet as she crossed the room. When she placed her hand on the latch, she felt a shiver of something between her and the Anywhere Door. Yanking on the Door, it swung open to reveal...a cave?

A small hole in the ceiling let in light while moss and ferns grew from the walls. A waterfall cascaded from the far wall, falling into a series of small pools before finally landing in a larger pool at the base. Wafts of steam came from the waterfall and pool, and warm air washed against her face. A stack of fluffy white towels sat on a rock shelf along with several bottles and jars.

"Oh, and this is the grotto where you can wash up, if you wish." Basil's face was flushing a deeper red.

Meg yawned and shut the Door. "I'll do that tomorrow. It isn't time for my weekly bath yet."

Basil shifted at that, looking away from her.

Strange. Meg opened the Door, and it once again led to the grotto. Stranger still.

She shut the Door, drew in a deep breath, and opened it again. Still the grotto.

"Come on, House. I want to go to bed." She slammed the Door this time, then jerked it open. Again, the Anywhere Door opened to the grotto. "Putrid possums! What is wrong with this Door? Why can't it open to just one room like a nice, normal door?"

Basil made a sound in the back of his throat. His face was red from the collar of his shirt all the way to the tips of his long, tapered ears. "I think the cottage is trying to tell you something."

"It's a house! How can it tell me anything? Please don't say the house actually has thoughts?" Meg let go of the Door, backing away a step. She had been prepared for a lot of strange things, but she wasn't about to stay inside a thinking, living house.

"The house isn't sentient or anything like that. It senses a need and does its best to fulfill that need." Basil gave that cleared throat noise again. "And the house is sensing that you need...you are...well, you are a tad...dirty."

Meg glanced down at herself. Dirt crusted between her toes while dust caked her dress. She sniffed at her sleeve. It did smell, a little. Not bad, though.

Then again, Basil smelled prim and proper as a posy. All clean and scented with some fancy odor she couldn't name.

If Basil and his house expected her to be clean, then that was what she'd do. She had to keep Basil happy and hope he either gave her enough money to pay off Cullen or she could find enough she could steal and sneak to her family.

"Fine, House. I'll take a bath." Meg reached for the Anywhere Door yet again.

Basil took a step forward, hesitated, then gestured to her. "When you're finished, you should be able to go straight through the Door into your room."

"Thanks." Meg turned back to him. "I mean that. Thanks. I…" Her throat closed, and she wasn't sure if she trusted him enough to spill the feelings building inside her chest. She had been braced to endure a lot at the hands of the fae who snatched her. Basil might not be the rich fae lord she'd hoped for, but he hadn't been cruel and demanding either. "Just…thanks."

Without looking at him, she hurried through the Door, stepping into the grotto.

As soon as the Anywhere Door closed behind her, the waterfall curled, then blasted her straight in the face.

Sputtering, Meg swiped at the water. "So much for not having thoughts. You're plenty peeved with me, aren't you, House? Well, then, I'm here. I'm taking a bath, just like you wanted."

Not that she smelled all that bad, but the House apparently picky.

After sliding the locking bolt, Meg scrubbed herself and her clothes all in one go, then peeled out of the wet clothes and placed them in the nook next to the towels. She hoped the dress would be somewhat dry by the time she finished her bath, since it was the only item of clothing she had to wear.

She gathered all of the bottles and jars in the nook. She wasn't sure what half the stuff was, but she scrubbed with all of it anyway. She didn't want the House getting peeved at her all over again because she missed some crucial step.

When Meg finished, she dried off and reached for her dress. As she picked it up, she froze.

This wasn't her dress. The fabric beneath her fingers was fully dry and clean. Instead of the threadbare, patched garment she had left in the nook, an entirely new outfit rested there.

Should she put it on? Somehow, it seemed dangerous to dress in something that magically appeared in this bathing grotto. What would happen if the House decided to make it disappear at a horribly inconvenient time?

What other choice did she have? Her old dress was nowhere to be seen, and she couldn't very well run around in nothing but a towel. That had also been supplied by the House.

Quickly, she pulled on the new dress. It had a wide neckline with a serviceable brown bodice that laced up the front. Its green sleeves reached her wrists while a matching green skirt fell just past her knees in multiple points and layers over thick leggings. A pair of leather boots laced up her calves, ending just below her knees.

The outfit was sensible, sturdy, and comfortable. Not seductive or revealing or anything she would have expected from the Fae Realm or this house, based on the stories of fae males seducing innocent human girls who wandered into the forest.

Perhaps this cantankerous House wasn't all bad. Did that

mean Basil wasn't like those fae in stories either? Could she trust the kindness he'd shown her so far?

Meg patted the wall. "Thank you, House, for the dress. It's perfect."

Was that a sense of smug satisfaction coming from the magic surrounding this place? Perhaps it was just Meg's imagination.

This time, when she opened the Anywhere Door, it didn't lead into the main room of the cottage but instead revealed the room Basil had said was hers. The sleeping nook she'd glimpsed before seemed even more inviting now. Once she was in the room, she could see a wardrobe set into the wall next to the nook, its doors crooked and covered with a layer of moss and tiny purple flowers.

She'd explore it more thoroughly in the morning. For now, all she wanted was rest. When she crawled into the sleeping nook, the blankets were soft and the moss mattress was far better than the straw tick at the home she'd left.

Perhaps she'd made the right choice in running to the forest, talking horses and sentient houses notwithstanding. Only time would tell.

Meg wasn't about to drop her guard yet. Not until she figured out exactly why her fae husband had decided to steal a human for his bride and what he wanted from her.

And until she could figure out how to get the gold she needed from him.

## CHAPTER 6

*M*eg slept surprisingly well, considering the strange bed and even stranger house.

Still, she forced herself to get up at what she guessed was the break of dawn here in this place. She wanted a chance to search the House for any hidden riches before Basil woke up. Assuming the House didn't have a way to tattle on her.

The House was slightly creepy, but it had provided a nice room and dress for her. When she peeked into the wardrobe, it was disappointingly empty. Still, one new dress and boots —real boots—were such a luxury.

After straightening her hair and dress, Meg stepped through the Anywhere Door, and it thankfully led her right into the kitchen rather than playing any tricks. Both the top and bottom half of Buddy's door remained closed, and Basil wasn't there yet.

Good. Maybe Meg would have a chance to search the cupboards and still have enough time to get breakfast started to keep up the appearance of a good, human bride.

Meg faced the few, oddly shaped cupboards that filled one wall. What would she find inside? Jars of eyeballs and gigantic spiders and severed fingers from the last human this fae snatched?

Meg drew her shoulders straight. Whatever was in these cupboards, she could handle it. "All right, House. No tricks. I'm just trying to make a spot of breakfast."

The House gave a grumpy little shuffle that creaked through the cupboard doors.

That wasn't reassuring. It had been so cooperative with the clothes. Could it tell she was partially lying about making breakfast?

Meg steeled herself and opened the first cupboard. Nothing jumped out at her. Then again, there didn't seem to be anything in the cupboard at all.

She opened the next cupboard. Still nothing in it.

Was this another trick of the House? Or were all these cupboards really empty? Meg gave a growl and yanked open one cupboard after the other. It was getting really annoying, never knowing what was real and what was a trick of this crazy House.

She stood back and planted her hands on her hips. No jewels or gold or anything sellable stashed away in here. There wasn't even any food, which didn't make sense for a kitchen.

The Anywhere Door gave a click behind her. She glanced up to find her fae husband Basil leaning in the doorway. His dark brown hair was tousled, the collar of his light gray shirt unbuttoned and opened wide enough to show off some of his chest. He carried a dark green coat over his arm.

He wasn't the epically muscular fae warrior she'd had in mind when she'd set out to be snatched, but his chiseled features and the way his dark hair fell across his forehead were handsome, in a nice, adorable kind of way.

She shook herself, her chest tightening. What was she thinking? His niceness could all be an act and if he realized she was succumbing to his charms, he would take advantage of her. She couldn't let her guard down. She had to focus on her mission to save her family.

She gestured to the cupboards. "Where do you find food in this place? Do you fae even eat?"

For a moment, Basil blinked at her like a sleepy raccoon caught out in daylight. Then, he set his coat on the back of one of the chairs, crossed the room, and reached for one of the cupboards. "All you have to do is ask the cottage, and food will appear in this cupboard. Just like the wardrobe in your room will provide your clothes for the day."

He didn't have to sound so snarky about that, as if she was unintelligent for not having figured out that the House was apparently capable of magicking food out of thin air. Even if she had seen evidence of how it whisked the clothes she was wearing into existence last night.

"Huh." Meg grimaced as she glared at the offending cupboards. "I'm not sure this House will listen to me."

"It will. We are bound, and thus the cottage is bound to you as much as it is to me." Basil gripped the cupboard's knob, using that frustratingly condescending voice, as if he didn't understand what her problem was with the House. "Breakfast, please."

When he opened the cupboard, it was filled with two baked pastries.

Of course the House cooperated for him. Meg peered at the food. "That was empty before. Don't know if I dare eat food this House whomped up."

"The cottage didn't create it. It just fetched the food from another Court." Basil pulled out the food and handed one of the pastries to her. After she took it, he retreated across the room and plopped into one of the chairs by the fireplace. As he sat, the fire flared to life, just a tiny crackle that was large enough to provide atmosphere.

This House was weird. Meg took the other chair by the fire. At least the chair was as comfortable as the mattress and the moss flooring.

She turned the pastry over in her hands. Did she dare eat it? "What do you mean, the House fetched the food?"

Fetching food from somewhere else in this crazy Realm didn't sound any better than creating it from thin air.

If anything, Basil's expression and tone turned even more lecturing. "The Court of Knowledge has agreements with many of the other courts. The other courts provide necessary food and clothing for people in our Court in exchange for access to our knowledge."

"Huh." Meg inspected the pastry for a few more seconds. Well, she had to eat. If this turned her into a blue rabbit or a pink squirrel or something else crazy, she didn't have much of a choice, any more than she had a choice to wear this outfit. Hopefully the House didn't try to poison her. Basil had better be correct about the magical binding protecting her as his mate.

Tentatively, she took a bite. Flavors burst across her tongue. She closed her eyes, savoring the taste. Sweet, yet tart like an apple. Though, it didn't taste like an apple. It was more like eating maple candy and pure sunshine.

When she opened her eyes to take a second bite, she frowned at the pastry. "What is this made of?"

Basil's face fell, almost as if he had been hoping for a different reaction. He glanced down at his own half-eaten pastry. The inside of his was purple and blue as well. "It's just fruit and nuts. None of them are ones that would still be dangerous for you to eat even with the binding to me."

A rustling came from inside Buddy's stall before his head poked over the lower door. He blinked sleepily at them. "Can the two of you keep it quiet out here? I'm trying to get my beauty sleep."

"Sorry." Basil glanced at Meg, as if expecting her to share in an inside joke. "Buddy tends to stay up half the night eating clover and then sleep most of the morning. So he only has himself to blame."

"You should be sorry. It is perfectly acceptable for a talking equine to stay up most of the night. Everyone knows clover tastes best by moonlight." Buddy shook his shaggy mane and glared at Basil. "I'm seriously rethinking telling you to get a mate if you're going to be this noisy in the mornings from now on."

Meg nearly choked on her pastry. "*You* told him to go snatch a mate?"

Why would the pony want Basil to go steal a bride?

Perhaps getting eaten by wolves there in the forest would have been the better option.

Buddy swung his head to focus on Meg. "He has been mopey and lonely, and it was starting to get pathetic."

Basil made a choking sound, then started coughing. Interestingly enough, his face had gone red as a strawberry. Maybe it was because he was choking. Or he could have been embarrassed.

Buddy kept right on speaking as if nothing was amiss. "So I talked him into snatching a human bride. He needed someone sensible. Are you sensible, human girl?"

Was she? Meg stared back at the talking pony. "I think so."

"I think so, too. After all, the House sensed your preference for a sturdy dress, and that's a good sign if I ever saw one." Buddy bobbed his head, flopping his shaggy mane across his broad forehead. "You'll do nicely."

She wasn't sure how to respond to that. After all, she had married the fae who had stolen her away in the middle of the night. She hadn't been all that sensible lately.

Instead, she ate the rest of her pastry in silence. There

was a lot they probably should talk about, but it was far too early in the morning for awkward conversations.

Besides, the pastry was too delicious to waste time talking. She hadn't turned into an animal yet, so she might as well enjoy it.

When she finished, she licked her fingers, crossed the room, and placed her hand on the cupboard's knob. "More breakfast, please."

When she opened the cupboard door, all that it contained was a hard crust of bread and a bit of moldy cheese.

Meg pointed. "Is that enough proof that your House doesn't like me much?"

Basil's eyebrows shot up as he glanced from her to the cupboard. "Maybe it didn't like your sticky fingers on the knob?"

Huffing and rolling her eyes, Meg scrubbed her fingers on her dress. "Annoying uppity House. There, you happy? Now, can I have more breakfast? Please?"

This time when she opened the cupboard, another pastry waited for her. She grinned, thanked the House since she might as well reward good behavior, and dug in with gusto. Whatever the inconveniences of this place, the food was excellent.

Basil was scrutinizing her with those deep eyes of his, staring long enough that she had to resist the urge to squirm. She did her best to ignore him.

After she finished her second meal in a few bites, she licked off her fingers and scrubbed them dry on her dress. As much as she didn't want to, it was time to start asking those awkward questions. "Well? What happens now? Do I stay here and cook or clean or something until you get back? What does a fae's mate do all day?"

In other words, what did Basil expect from her? Whatever it was, she would do her best to fulfill it. The happier he was with her, the more likely he was to shower her with gold or jewels, if he had any.

Basil stared down at his hands, his hair falling across his forehead. "There's no need to cook, as you can see, and the cottage keeps itself clean. So you'll work in the Great Library with me. This is the Court of Knowledge. Our entire Court is centered around our Great Library." When Basil lifted his gaze to hers, his voice was filled with something like pride.

It was Meg's turn to gape. Was Basil serious? He wanted her to work…at a library?

This could be a problem. Her entire village didn't have one book between them. Books didn't put food in their bellies, a roof over their heads, or pay off Cullen.

Did she dare tell Basil that she couldn't even read? What would he do? Would he decide she was no longer any use to him and dump her back where he'd found her? Back in the faerie circle in the forest where she would be eaten by wolves or, worse, taken away by Cullen.

No, she couldn't tell Basil. She would have to fake it and hope she could fool him. Creepy houses and annoying talking horses aside, this was the best situation she had ever found herself in. She had a cushy bed and a full stomach. She couldn't do anything to risk losing that. Especially not if she wanted to save her siblings.

Meg faced Basil and pasted on the sweetest smile she could manage. "Sounds…exciting. Is this Library all alive and stuff just like the creepy House?"

The whole House gave a huffy shudder. A shower of dirt came from the ceiling and dropped on Meg's head.

Meg brushed at her hair and glared. Annoying, kind-of-alive House.

Basil scowled up at the ceiling as well before turning his gaze back to her. "Just a suggestion. Don't go insulting the

Great Library when we're there. The cottage might get huffy, but the Library could actually hurt you if it doesn't like you."

"Great. That's just great." This Library sounded *so* pleasant. Pretending to like working in a library to please her new fae husband and this snooty library might be more complicated than she thought.

But she didn't have a choice. Right now, she just needed to keep Basil happy, make sure he kept giving her food and shelter, and eventually figure out a way to mine the riches of this realm.

She shoved to her feet. "Well, let's see this Library of yours."

Buddy gave another snort. "Yes, Basil. Please get going. If you don't, I'm going to use the Anywhere Door first to get to the clover glade."

"Fine, fine. We're leaving." Basil popped to his feet, brushed off his trousers, and picked up his coat. When he shrugged into it, the coat hugged his shoulders and fell to his knees, emphasizing his fine figure.

Meg shook herself. Enough staring. She needed to keep her wits about her.

As if unaware that Meg was gawking at him, Basil crossed the room and reached for the Anywhere Door. "Sometimes I like to walk and enjoy the morning, but I think I'd like to use the extra time to get you settled in and show you the Library."

Bracing herself, she joined him standing next to the Door. Time to see this fancy Library of his.

"Ready?" He gave her a grin.

She forced herself to grin back. If feigned enthusiasm about a library could keep the food coming, then she would give the best performance of her life.

He gripped the latch. "Take us to the Great Library."

When he opened the Door, a white light flooded into the room.

Meg squinted into the brightness as Basil tugged her forward. She stumbled at his side, her boots going from spongy moss to smooth stone. As her eyes adjusted, she found herself standing in a grand hall, all in a white stone veined with black and gray. White pillars shaped like gnarled trees held up the roof. The roof itself was mostly windows, beaming sunlight down into the hall.

The hall itself was filled with a bustle of people. Well, fae. Many were like Basil, with slim faces and long, tapered ears. Some with a tuft of fur at the ends of their ears or others without, like Basil. Some had a variety of tails. Long, monkey-like tails or bushy fox tails.

Tiny, gray-skinned creatures scuttled quickly out of the way. Several tall, tree-like figures strolled through the bustle, shedding leaves from their hair.

Between the pillars, arched doorways lined the two long sides of the hall, occasionally opening and shutting to admit more fae. Each of the narrow ends of this grand hall contained even larger gate-like doors several stories tall.

The bustle seemed to generally move in one direction, headed for the massive doors to the right. They didn't form an orderly queue, exactly, but the suggestion of one was there.

"All the doors along this entrance hall are Anywhere Doors. They connect to the homes of other librarians, both the ones who work here and the librarians across the entire Court of Knowledge." Next to her, Basil's tone turned into that lecturing one again. "They also connect to all of the Courts in the Fae Realm so that members of those Courts can seek the knowledge we provide and so that we can visit those Courts both to give knowledge and to find more books and information to add to the Great Library."

She was probably supposed to be impressed. But all she could think was that this was an awful lot of magic and work for something as inedible as books.

Meg cleared her throat. "Is it always this busy?"

Something in Basil's expression fell, though as he swept a glance over the hall again, he frowned. "Must be the Midsummer rush. Come on. I need to report in."

Meg let him tug her through the crowd of fae. She kept her head down, not meeting anyone's gazes even under the prickle of stares.

The tall fae women guarding the doors were dressed in leather and plates of armor. Their leather skirts ended just above their knees while boots laced up their calves. Both had swords strapped at their waists.

After one glance at Basil, the warrior women let him and Meg past without any hassle.

Basil leaned closer to Meg. "The Court of Swordmaidens is providing security for the Great Library, now that our court's king will soon marry their queen."

Meg could only nod as she edged nearer to Basil. Not that she felt particularly safe around him, but he was less scary than those imposing warrior women fae with their massive swords and stern expressions.

The doors opened to another vast space, this one carpeted with the familiar moss. Instead of the white marble, this room was all living wood, just like the inside of Basil's cottage. A massive tree stood in the center of the hall beneath the curving, glass dome set into the ceiling. The tree's spreading branches and blue-green leaves reached high above the room and muted the light.

Books filled the walls from the floor all the way to the ceiling, with walkways and ladders providing access to the books on the higher stories. Winding shelves spiraled around the edges of the room, all of them packed with books. Doorways branched into more wings and rooms.

A circle of desks was built into the roots of the tree and was manned by fae wearing gray shirts and coats identical to Basil's, except that their coats were black instead of green.

The fae who had been admitted by the stern-faced women were lined up in front of each of the desks. Others, dressed as Basil was in gray shirts and green coats, bustled back and forth from the winding shelves to the desks and back again.

Now Meg understood why the warrior women had allowed Basil past without asking for identification. Those coats were the uniform for the librarians who worked at the Great Library. The different colors must signal status of some sort.

Basil reached for her, then withdrew his hand, as if he didn't dare touch her. "Well, this is the Great Library. Isn't it amazing?"

It looked downright terrifying. All those books, and she couldn't read a lick.

Of all fae to steal her, why did she have to get snatched by a librarian?

CHAPTER 7

*B*asil was one big knot of nerves. As he forced himself to walk toward the desks to report in, his stomach churned so much he thought he might lose his breakfast right there in the middle of the Library.

That would make a *great* impression on his new wife.

His wife.

What in all the Realms had he been thinking last night? Sure, the Midsummer Revel was coming up, and with Lysander and Hermia running off that night, and Demetrius likely to follow with his faithful shadow Helena tagging after him, Basil would need the help at the Library to defend it against monsters.

But was a human really the best option? If he'd wanted help fighting off monsters, he should have followed King Theseus's example and convinced a bride from the Court of Swordmaidens to marry him.

Though—he glanced over his shoulder at the two swordmaidens guarding the doors to the Library—he never would have gotten up the courage to approach one of them, much less attempt to snatch one.

Stealing a human had been a lot simpler, especially since Meg had been waiting in the circle for him. He would have to hope she was enough. He was stuck with her now.

She trotted at his side as he circled the desks to avoid running into Master Librarian Domitius. Instead, he approached the desk manned by Head Librarian Marco.

"Basil, good, you're here. As you can see, we are rather busy this morning." Head Librarian Marco glanced up as they approached and gestured to the line, getting his hand caught in his beard. He tugged his hand free, wincing. "And who is this?"

Basil glanced at Meg, his tongue feeling thick as he managed to choke out, "This is Meg. My…wife."

"Good. You'll need her. This Midsummer Night is shaping up to be a chaotic one." Head Librarian Marco swept a glance over Meg, then gave a sharp nod. "Welcome to the Great Library, Meg. I'm sure you'll fit right in. Basil, Puck is already here, if you wouldn't mind handling his request."

Basil stifled a groan. Everyone hated dealing with Puck. If he wasn't up to mischief of his own, he was running mischief-related errands for King Oberon of the Court of Revels. Either way, he always caused trouble. For everyone.

"I'll handle him." Basil scanned the bustling atrium of the Library and spotted Puck's small figure loitering on one of the shelves. Not a good sign.

Basil headed in Puck's direction with Meg at his side.

The sprite perched on one of the upper shelves, his leaf loincloth barely covering the essentials. He was blithely yanking books from the shelf and tossing them at the heads of those passing by.

Around him, the Library shook, as if trying to dislodge him from his perch high on the shelves. A sense of annoyance turning to anger pressed around them, shadows growing in the corners.

Puck reached for yet one more book, but a branch from the bookshelf snapped forward and swatted the sprite from the shelf.

The moss rippled, shifting the pile of books out of the way before Puck landed on the floor, his loincloth riding up, before he bounced to his feet with a flourish. Even at full height, he didn't even come up to Basil's waist. His white hair flared around his head while two tiny nubs of horns poked through the mess. His ears were tapered with clumps of hair at the ends while a tiny tuft of a beard sprouted from his chin, a shock of white against his green skin.

Basil crossed his arms and glared at the sprite. "Stop aggravating the Library. It might decide to eat you one of these days."

Puck smirked and bowed. "Librarian Basil. A pleasure as always. I do believe if the Library was capable of eating people, it would have done so to me long before now."

The shelves behind Puck shuddered for a moment, as if the Great Library was giving an annoyed huff.

Meg edged closer to Basil, her eyes wide as she glanced from Puck to the shelves and back.

Basil would have reassured her, but he didn't want to say anything in front of Puck. He didn't even put an arm around her shoulders or a hand on her arm.

It was best not to give Puck—and thus King Oberon and Queen Titania—anything to toy with. They weren't supposed to mess with those in other Courts but that didn't always stop them.

Between the marital strife that periodically divided the Court of Revels and the way that same marital strife wore thin spots into the Realm of Monsters, it was a dangerous time to share a border with that particular Court.

Something in Basil's stance or Meg's movement still must have alerted Puck. His gaze swung to Meg, and his smirk widened, showing off rows of slightly sharp teeth. "And who is this? A new friend of yours? Or"—Puck's tone turned suggestive—"more than a friend?"

Basil wasn't about to answer that. "How can I help you today, Puck? Or, more likely, how can I help King Oberon?" Basil worked to keep his tone as formal and neutral as possible.

"Touchy topic, I can see. Fine, I won't ask about the human girl. For now." Puck kicked at one of the books lying on the moss floor, though the Library shifted the book out of the way at the last second. Scowling, Puck returned his attention back to Basil. "My King Oberon is in need of a love spell. One he hasn't used before. Perhaps an enchanted plant this time?"

Basil held out his hand. "Do you have the proper forms?"

Puck pulled a roll of paper out of his leaf loincloth.

Where he had room to store a large roll of paper in such a scanty piece of clothing, Basil didn't know and wasn't about to ask. All that truly mattered was getting the forms.

Smirking, Puck peeled the top paper from the roll. "Here is the form that states that His Majesty King Oberon understands that the Great Library is not responsible for any repercussions of how he uses this information. Here is the form that states that King Oberon really and truly understands that the Library is not responsible for how he uses any information learned here. And here is the form that states that King Oberon will not use this information on anyone in another Court. This form states that King Oberon has not lied on any of these forms. And, finally, here is the form, which states that King Oberon himself—the real King Oberon, not a decoy, actor, or impersonator—actually signed all these forms."

It was a wad of paper, but Basil had the sinking feeling that it still wouldn't be enough. King Oberon—and his queen

Titania whenever she asked for information from the Great Library—always found a way to weasel out of all the restrictions.

This was the duty of the Court of Knowledge and the Great Library. They had an obligation to give information whenever asked, no matter who was doing the asking.

"Very well." Basil tucked the papers into one of many inside pockets of his coat. He would hold onto them until he had a chance to add them to the room filled with similar stacks of signed forms from the rulers of the Court of Revels.

Basil hesitated, glancing between Meg and Puck, who was bouncing on his toes and reaching for a book on the shelf before the Library shuffled the book away from his grasping fingers.

"Meg, could you please help the Library put the books away?" Basil didn't wait for her response. Getting Puck the requested information and on his way was far more pressing. "Puck, if you would please follow me."

Basil led the way deeper into the Great Library, weaving his way between the bookshelves. He kept Puck in sight because, well, he was Puck. There was no telling what trouble he could get into if left unsupervised for even a second.

In the section on magical plants, Basil halted below the tall shelves built into the wall. "Library, could you please find me a book with magical plants used in love spells?"

The shelves gave a shiver, then a branch detached itself. It plucked a book from one of the higher shelves, then held it out to Basil.

Basil took the book from the branch, then leafed through it until he found a purple flower whose nectar caused love if dripped into someone's eye. The next page over was for a white flower that was an antidote for the purple one. Perfect.

Puck clambered up the shelves and leaned over precariously to peer at the book as well. "Oh, that should do nicely."

"Do I even want to know what King Oberon intends to do with this?" Basil withdrew two blank pieces of paper from another pocket of his coat.

"Nope." Puck grinned and hopped to the ground.

This wasn't going to end well. King Oberon was probably going to tear a hole in the barrier with the Realm of Monsters with his antics. But if Basil refused to give Puck the requested information, that action would go against the code of the Court of Knowledge and was just as likely to cause a thin spot.

He had no choice but to do his job. If he started to withhold information because he feared what someone *might* do with that knowledge, he would never stop. He was only responsible for giving knowledge. He had no responsibility for how someone chose to use that knowledge once given.

Placing one of his blank pieces of paper on the page about the purple love flower, Basil drew on the magic of the Library. With a shiver, the book page was duplicated onto the formerly blank paper.

He did the same for the page on the antidote flower. When he was finished, he handed both pages to Puck. "Now, remember—"

"I know. I am to hand these pages to only King Oberon and no one else. I shouldn't lose them or forget to hand them over. Yada, yada." Puck waved his free hand airily. "You give me this speech every time. Don't know why you bother."

"I keep hoping you'll listen one of these days. We'd all be a lot safer if that happened." Basil closed the book and held it out to the waiting branch. "Please return the book to its place."

The Library obligingly placed the book on the shelf,

giving it a small pat with the branch as if satisfied the book was safely restored to its spot.

"Where's the fun in that?" Puck flounced off into the shelves. In the wrong direction.

"Puck…" Basil pointed back the way they had come.

With a pout, Puck turned on his heel and marched in an exaggerated fashion toward the exit, each step hiking the leaf loincloth in a way that Basil was not comfortable seeing.

Basil escorted Puck all the way to the Grand Hall of Anywhere Doors, watching until Puck stepped through a Door to make sure Puck left.

As Basil stepped back into the Library's atrium, a scream echoed against the glass dome.

Everyone halted what they were doing, turning toward the shelves where Basil had left Meg.

Basil's heart clenched. Meg. He'd left her alone. What if she'd done something to anger the Library? Or a monster had somehow gotten into the Library even before Midsummer Night?

Basil broke into a run, shoving between two nymphs waiting in line. As he raced past, Master Librarian Domitius scowled, but Marco's eyebrows lifted, and a smile twitched at his long white beard.

Another screech rang out, this one more a war cry than a scream.

Basil skidded around a corner and came to an abrupt halt at the sight before him.

Meg balanced on the pile of books Puck had tossed from the shelves. Four thin branches reached down from the shelves, grasping for her, while she dodged and batted them away with the book she clutched in both hands. Her blonde hair frizzed around her head, a few strands clinging to the end of one of the snatching branches.

At the base of the pile of books, a circle of five bookwyrms hissed and growled, their leather ruffs puffed out in a menacing fashion. When one of them started to slither up the stack of books toward Meg, she kicked at it. "Stay away, you monsters! Back!"

Even as Basil stood there, another two bookwyrms joined the others.

Not good. Apparently Meg had managed to do something to annoy the Library.

"Just calm down." Basil edged closer. He wasn't sure if he was telling that to the Library, the bookwyrms, or Meg. All three, actually.

Meg's head snapped up. "Basil! These dragons just started attacking me. As did the Library." She ducked and parried a whipping branch.

"Set the book down. Gently." Basil nudged aside a few of the hissing, snarling bookwyrms. "The Library and book-wyrms think you're a danger."

"*I'm* a danger? They're the ones attacking me!" Meg's fingers tightened on the book she held, her voice going an octave higher.

The bookwyrms hissed, their forked red tongues flicking in and out.

Meg scrambled higher on the pile of books.

This wasn't going well. Basil rushed forward and scooped Meg up in his arms, hauling her from the pile of books and out of range of the Library's branches.

She let out a piercing shriek, but she didn't try to squirm out of his grip. She still clutched the book, hugging it to her chest like a shield.

The branches stopped waving about and instead rested on the empty shelves, almost like the Library had crossed its arms. One branch tapped against a shelf, impatient.

"Meg, the Library wants its book back." Basil resisted the

urge to adjust his grip on her, not sure what to do, now that she was in his arms.

She raised her arm as if preparing to toss the book.

"No! No, don't throw it!" Basil nearly dropped her, torn between holding her and stopping her from angering the Library further.

"Well, what am I supposed to do with it?" Meg glared at him.

This close, her eyes were an interesting color of brown. Rich and vibrant with flecks of gold and amber in them. Such strangely fascinating eyes…

She whacked his chest with the book. "You just rushed off and said something about helping the Library shelve the books, but you didn't explain how I was supposed to do that. Nor did you explain about them." She jabbed the book in the direction of the bookwyrms.

All seven of the bookwyrms perched on the curves of their tails. Two of them still had their ruffs extended, but most of them had relaxed, even if they lined up between the stack of books and Basil and Meg.

"Sorry." He hadn't done a good job of looking after her. This was not only her first day here at the Library, but also her first day in the Fae Realm. Of course she would be confused.

He didn't know a whole lot about being a husband—this was his first day at this marriage thing as well—but he knew he should have done a better job. If Buddy hadn't badgered him into snatching a human bride at the last moment, he would have taken his time to do his research first. Surely the Library had information on humans, their customs, and their realm. The Library might even have knowledge on how to be a proper husband.

Meg scowled, her glare sharpening.

Right. Explanations.

"Normally, when you take one book off the shelf, the Library can return it easily enough. But Puck tossed so many books off the shelves that it helps the Library if you read off the title when you ask the Library to put it back." Basil eased Meg back to her feet. He picked up one of the books. "Library, could you please put away *Notes on the Care of Toadstools?*"

The Library snaked down one branch and plucked the book from his grip. After placing the book in its spot on one of the upper shelves, the branch gave a smug pat to the book's spine.

"Now you give it a try with your book." Basil gave Meg what he hoped was an encouraging smile.

She held up the book, her scowl deepening. "I can't read it."

Basil glanced from her to the book and back. "Really? You should be able to because of the binding, the same way you can understand the fae language."

Her jaw clenched, and she spat between gritted teeth, "I *can't* read."

Oh. *Oh.* It had never occurred to him that she just plain couldn't read. Even the lowliest fae in the Court of Knowledge could read.

What was he going to do? He had a wife who was supposed to help him in the Library, but she couldn't read. That was what he got for snatching the first human girl he came across. He had known this was a bad idea from the moment Buddy suggested it.

No time to think about that now. Meg was still giving him that scowl, and she had quite the impressive glower.

"In that case, if you could hand the books to me, I'll read off the titles for the Library." Basil hoped he disguised his disappointment.

"What about them?" Meg gestured toward the bookwyrms.

"We just need to show them you aren't a threat to the books." Basil knelt, then tugged Meg down next to him. "The bookwyrms guard the Library."

When he extended his hand, a dark blue bookwyrm slithered closer and nuzzled into his palm. He scratched around the wyrm's ruff until it let out a rumbling purr, far deeper and raspier than a cat's.

"Seems a bit risky, having dragons guard a library." Meg remained at Basil's side, though she didn't hold out her hand to any of the bookwyrms.

"They aren't dragons, exactly. They're wyrms. They don't breathe fire, only hot air, which helps them keep the Library dry enough for the books." Basil stroked the blue wyrm's back as two more bookwyrms wiggled closer to beg for his attention. "These are the younger ones, and they help guard the main floor. The larger, older wyrms guard the towers where the dangerous books are kept."

Meg's eyebrows shot up. "Dangerous books? How can a book be dangerous?"

Basil shrugged. "Grimoires filled with deadly spells that even the fae don't dare utter. Tomes that have gotten a mind of their own and are a bit more alive than a book ought to be. Books that can drag people inside the story and trap them there. Ancient scrolls that hold curses best forgotten. That sort of thing. Only Master Librarians are allowed to enter the towers, though Head Librarian Marco gave me a tour when I gained my position here."

"Oh good. Alive books and giant worms. That's great. Just great," Meg muttered under her breath. "Wolves definitely would have been the better option."

Basil ignored her. She didn't seem to require a response.

She was odd. Mildly unmannerly. He'd thought a mate

would give him someone sensible at his side, not add to the chaos.

Footsteps brushed against the moss behind Basil. When he glanced over his shoulder, he found Master Librarian Domitius glaring at him, arms crossed. "The Library is busier than ever, and here you are flirting with your new wife instead of working. Do you want this job or not? Now get back to work. Clean up this mess."

Basil gritted his teeth and pushed to his feet. "Yes, sir. Right away, sir."

As Basil leaned down and picked up a book, the worst part was seeing the pitying look on Meg's face. If he'd thought stealing a human bride would gain him prestige, he had been wrong. Even in her eyes, he couldn't manage to be a mysterious fae warrior. Instead, he was still the same scholarly assistant librarian he had always been.

eg's face hurt from holding her fake smile all day. After the debacle with the bookwyrms and her inability to read, she had helped Basil re-shelve all the books that the crazy sprite Puck had tossed off the shelves. Then she had awkwardly trailed after Basil as he was sent back and forth across the Library fetching books and information for the master librarians.

By the time she and Basil stepped through the Anywhere Door into his House, her feet were sore, her shoulders ached, and she was beginning to think that staying back in her world might not have been so awful after all.

"Are you hungry? I will ask the cupboard for food." Basil shifted, standing in the center of the cottage's main room. His dark hair fell across his forehead, and he looked rather forlorn.

But Meg was in no mood for making nice. "Not hungry."

She spun on her heel and reached for the latch to the Anywhere Door. Before she could touch it and ask to be brought to her room, the Door opened.

Buddy, the talking pony companion, trotted through. Behind him, Meg caught a glimpse of a shadowed glade formed of a draping willow tree in an odd blue-green color and a bubbling stream bordered by a swathe of clover and thick grass before the Door swung shut behind him.

She wasn't sure she wanted to know how the talking pony managed to open the Anywhere Door.

Buddy glanced between Meg and Basil. "I'm seeing a lot of long faces around here, and I'm not just talking about mine. Terrible day? Were the Foolish Four up to no good?"

"Actually, none of them even bothered to show up to work today." Basil scratched the back of his neck, looking even more dejected.

Meg wasn't buying it. She was done with all the confusion and strangeness of this place. She just wanted to go home to her family, to her normal world where houses didn't have a mind of their own and libraries didn't shelve books by themselves. She didn't want to ask who the Foolish Four were or why they weren't working at the Library.

She couldn't handle any of this anymore. She placed her hand on the latch to the Door. "Take me to my room."

When she opened the Door, it showed the grotto.

"Don't you *dare* do this to me. Not today." Meg slammed the Door, a lump forming in the back of her throat. At this point, she wasn't sure if that lump would turn into tears or a scream if she gave in. "Open to my room or so help me, I will burn this whole place to the ground. Got that, House?"

The House gave a shiver, but when Meg opened the Door, it led to the cozy, moss-blanketed room she had been given.

Without a glance toward Buddy or Basil, Meg stomped through and flung the Door shut behind her.

The House gave another shudder, yanking on the moss beneath her feet so that she stumbled.

Ticking off the House was probably the last thing Meg needed right now. But she didn't care.

Her life was a mess. She had run from home trying to escape a bad situation but had only landed herself into an even worse one. She'd thought she would be fine, as long as she was provided with food and clothing.

But it turned out she wanted more. She had run because she'd clung to the last shred of hope that wherever she would end up would be better than what she had left.

But that hope was now gone. She was stuck in this weird realm where nothing operated the way it should. She was expected to work in a *library* of all things when she couldn't even read. She had no idea what was going on or what she was supposed to do.

Clearly, Basil wasn't a fae lord. He didn't have any gold or riches she could use to pay off Cullen. Her siblings were far away and in danger, and she was stuck here with no way to rescue them.

Forget about all her grand plans of a better life. Forget about love with that fae husband of hers.

Why was she even thinking about love?

Meg curled on the soft bed in the nook, buried her face in the pillow, and let herself cry.

After a moment, the Door creaked open. Apparently Basil hadn't taken the hint and had followed her inside.

The last thing she wanted to do was see him. "Go away! I don't want to talk right now."

"Then we won't talk. You can hug my neck and cry into my mane. I am told it is rather soothing," Buddy said, a moment before the soft clopping of hooves on moss filled the room.

Meg lifted her head and swiped the end of her sleeve over her face. "What are you doing here?"

Buddy stood in the center of the room, his dark brown

coat sleek and gleaming even in the dull half-light. He stuck his head into the nook. "I am a talking equine companion. Providing comfort and companionship is part of my job description."

She didn't want to like anything in this place. And she probably should blame Buddy for giving Basil the advice to snatch a human bride in the first place.

But it was hard to stay angry at Buddy when he was looking at her with those huge, deep brown eyes of his.

She wrapped her arms around his thick neck and buried her face against his soft coat. Drawing in a deep breath, she inhaled his musky, horse scent.

Buddy eased closer so that he could rest his head over her shoulder, as if giving her a hug. As he promised, he didn't talk. He just stood there. Solid and warm and surprisingly soft.

Meg sniffled as she leaned her head against the base of his broad neck, his coat warm against her cheek. A few more tears trickled down her cheeks, but she found herself relaxing and shuddering her way into silence rather than bursting into more sobs.

When she swiped at her face again, something white and fluttering dropped from the ceiling to land on the bed next to her. A handkerchief, provided by the House.

Meg took it, cleaned the tears from her face, then blew her nose. An attempt at a smile twitched on her face. "Is this the part where you offer that wise advice talking pony companions are supposed to have?"

"Of course." Buddy took a step back, regarding her with his deep liquid eyes. "I get the feeling that you're running from something. I'm not judging. Running is an instinctive reaction for equines as well. A blade of grass twitches the wrong way, and we take off for home at a dead run."

Meg drew up her knees, missing Buddy's warmth. He was

very huggable. And it was either talk to him or to Basil. Right now, the pony seemed like the safer option. "What do you do when home is the thing you're running from?"

"That is a rotten apple of a situation, for certain." Buddy blew a long breath over her face, and the warmth was somehow soothing. "Running will only get you so far. Eventually, you'll have to stop running and start building a new home. It will be tempting to keep running, since that is the far easier option. But if you're willing to make the sacrifices necessary, creating a new home is worth the effort."

Meg rested a hand on Buddy's broad forehead. "You know, that actually was wise advice."

"Of course it was. Didn't I tell you about my wisdom?" Buddy raised his head, a haughty look on his face, if a horse could look haughty. After a moment, he bumped her with his nose. "Can I tell you a secret?"

Why would he tell her a secret? Meg shrugged. "Sure."

"Basil is running, too, though he doesn't know it." With that, Buddy turned around—no small feat in the small bedroom, given his four legs and size—and trotted back out the Door that opened for him.

The Door swung shut behind him, though it didn't close all the way.

Basil's voice drifted through the opening. "How is she?"

Why hadn't the Door closed all the way? It was almost as if the House wanted Meg to eavesdrop.

Since eavesdropping was the House's idea, Meg slipped off the bed and tiptoed across the room. She peeked through the crack between the jamb and the Door.

Basil slumped in one of the chairs by the fire, head resting in his hands.

Something in Meg's chest squeezed just a little at seeing him looking so miserable.

Buddy trotted to him and nudged him with his nose. "Give her space. The Fae Realm is a lot to take in. And you weren't the most forthcoming today. Odd for you, given your propensity to lecture. I suggest that you have a good long chat with her tomorrow."

Basil groaned into his hands. "I blame you. This was all your idea."

"Don't blame me if you were desperate enough to try it." Buddy snorted at what little of Basil's face was visible around his hands. "And don't blame me if you fae are utterly illogical in your customs for finding a mate. Stealing a mate or participating in a Revel in a forest. Such a mess."

Basil glanced up, a hint of a smile playing across his mouth. "As if you talking equines are much better. You gather once a year as a herd, the stallions pose and snort and prance about to impress the mares, then each mare picks a stallion to be her lifelong mate purely based on looks."

"Hey, it isn't all based on looks. You can tell a lot about someone based on how they choose to show off." Buddy turned and headed toward his stall. As he passed Basil, Buddy swatted him in the face with his tail. "A tip for when you have that long overdue discussion with Meg. Ask her why she wanted to be snatched."

The Door eased shut, cutting off Meg's view and preventing her from hearing whatever Basil might have said in reply.

Meg leaned against the wall next to the Door, then slid down to sit on the moss-covered floor.

What was she supposed to do with the information that the House made sure she overheard? With her out of the room, Basil had no reason to act defeated and miserable, if that was just part of an act to win her over.

No, the emotions she had just witnessed had been

genuine. Basil truly felt terrible about how awful the day had been.

And, honestly, she shouldn't have gotten so frustrated with him. None of this was his fault, exactly. He had been following the customs of his people. Nor had he truly kidnapped her, since she had gone to that faerie circle intending to get herself stolen away by a fae. It had been her choice to end up here in this strange place.

Buddy was right. She had run from the situation back home—and run as far as she possibly could. When she couldn't run any farther, she had kept Basil—and even the House and the Great Library—at arm's length, trying to get them to run from her since she couldn't run from them.

But she could run no farther. This was her home and her life now. Basil, fae librarian and all, was her husband. It was time to stop running and start building.

What would that mean for her sisters and brother? Even if she built a life here with Basil, she couldn't abandon her siblings. She had promised that she would come back to them, bringing them enough money to save them from Cullen.

Perhaps she would have to talk to Basil about their situation. Maybe he knew of a way to obtain gold or riches here in the Fae Realm. Would he have enough clout with his king to ask for something like that?

Meg hugged herself. She would face Basil in the morning. For now, she might as well start with the House. It had been oddly kind to her in the past few minutes.

Tipping her head back, Meg stared at the ceiling, which seemed to be a woven network of branches. "All right, House. Let's call a truce. I know we didn't get off to the right start, and I'm sorry for whatever I've done to anger you. You are loyal to Basil. I get that. But, I guess, I'd like to get to know him better, and maybe be loyal to him as well. Got that?"

The House gave a small shake. Then, the moss floor lifted, sliding Meg onto the bed.

She managed to swallow back her shriek, and instead forced herself to smile. "Thank you, House."

The warmth that filled the room seemed almost smug.

## CHAPTER 9

The next morning, Basil braced himself before leaving his room. After the disaster that yesterday had turned out to be, he needed today to go well. They only had two days until Midsummer Night, and he still had to explain all that to Meg. She ought to know she would soon be facing an onslaught of monsters.

When he crept out of his room, he found Meg bustling around the kitchen. Instead of the scowls and slamming cupboards of the day before, this morning she smiled as she pulled an entire tray filled with food from the cupboard. The cupboard door even gave a little waggle, as if in pleasure, as she patted it. "Thank you, House."

Basil blinked. Blinked again.

Nope, the sight hadn't changed.

Had he stepped into an alternate realm? This was not what he was expecting to wake up to this morning.

What if the cottage had slipped faerie fruit to Meg while Basil wasn't looking? Basil hurried forward, heart suddenly tight in his chest.

Meg glanced up and smiled. *Smiled.* "Good morning, Basil."

"What did you eat this morning? Did the cottage slip you any fruit? Please tell me you didn't eat any fruit." Basil yanked the tray from her hands, scanning its contents. Large eggs with yellow-green yolks, a bowl of pink porridge topped with several purple berries, and slices of green toast. Nothing suspicious or dangerous for Meg.

Meg gaped at him for a moment. "No, I haven't eaten anything yet. I was going to wait for you. Why do you ask?"

"You're acting *nice*." Basil glanced from her to the tray in his hands and back again.

She winced, her face twisting. Her gaze fell to the tray. "Sorry about yesterday. I wasn't...I wasn't at my best, and I lashed out at you when I shouldn't have. I'm sorry for that."

"And I'm sorry I wasn't better at explaining and making the transition easier for you." Basil cleared his throat, the words coming out surprisingly rough. "I should have realized how difficult it would be, finding yourself in this realm."

The moss beneath Basil's feet sprouted a field of buds that burst into tiny white flowers.

He glanced down at the floor, raising his eyebrows. First the Anywhere Door only opened to the grotto, then the food cupboard refused to work for her. Now this. The cottage had never acted like this before. It wasn't sentient. It couldn't have feelings that could be hurt. Nor could it feel satisfaction when something went right.

Though, it was semi-sentient. Sort of. It was less sentient than the Great Library was, but it still had that sensing presence to it. Basil had read about how cottages could gain more of a personality, if treated as if they had one, the way Meg had been doing. The Great Library tended to take on some of the personality of its Head Librarians over the years.

Meg also glanced at the flower-covered floor, then her

smile widened. "I guess the House is happy with our apologies. Now let's eat so we can get to the Library on time."

Basil wasn't going to argue with that logic. They ate quickly, finishing just as Buddy poked his head over the lower half of the door, blinking at the light and grumbling about being awake.

As Basil and Meg strolled together toward the Anywhere Door, he had the strange impulse to reach for her hand.

When they stepped through the Door, the grand hall was quieter than it had been the day before, as if most people had hurried to get their needed information and now were staying well clear of the Library as Midsummer Night approached.

Not a good sign if fae from all over the Realm didn't want to go near their Court this Midsummer Night.

As they strolled into the Library, Basil circled near the edge of the atrium, trying to stay out of sight. He kept his voice low to avoid bringing attention to them, not daring to look at Meg. "I can show you the book repair room, and you can work on fixing books today, if you'd like. It involves sewing new bookbindings and activating the Library's magic, so you don't need to know how to read or have magic of your own."

He peeked at her as they entered the maze of shelves. He'd given it some thought last night, trying to think of something here at the Library that would help her feel useful. Was he presuming too much?

A smile curved her mouth and brightened her brown eyes. "Sewing? With a needle and thread and everything?"

"Yes. It's a special needle and sturdy thread, but I believe the general concept is the same." Basil gave a shrug, his own smile tugging on his face. "My parents started me out on basic mending before I was ever taught how to bind a book."

"Well, I have plenty of practice with mending." Meg

grinned, her steps lighter and quicker than Basil had yet seen. Not even the grandness of the Library had brought such a sparkle to her eyes as the thought of getting her hands on something as practical as a needle and thread.

In a far corner of the Library, the book repair room was tucked next to the stairs that led up to one of the towers of dangerous books. Stacks upon stacks of damaged books waited for attention, giving off a musty, old-book scent. Several tables with chairs filled the center of the room, scattered with half-repaired books, while a high window beamed light into the room.

A few bookwyrms scuttled through the shadows, their scales rasping against the book covers. The terrified squeak of some rodent pierced the quiet, followed by the sounds of a bookwyrm chomping it, adding to the feel of death and neglect.

Meg's eyes widened as she turned in a slow circle, taking in all the books. "Rabid rabbits, that's a lot of broken books. Did Puck get loose in the Library or something?"

"Puck damaged a few. Some are here just from the regular wear and tear of use." Basil shifted, unable to meet her gaze. "But most were damaged in monster attacks here at the Library."

"Monsters." Her tone was flat, and when he glanced up at her, she had her hands on her hips.

"Yes. I promise I'll give you a full explanation tonight." As much as she deserved to hear everything as soon as possible, Basil would rather tell her once they were home and wouldn't be interrupted.

After a moment, Meg nodded. "I'll hold you to that. For now, I just have one question. Was all this damage from one monster attack or several?"

He could see why she would ask. There were piles of books—probably several thousand books—waiting for repair. He would be scared, too, if all this was from a single monster.

Though, with the way this Midsummer Night was shaping up, there really could be this much destruction caused in one night.

But he wasn't ready to tell her that yet. She would need the freedom to be able to stomp away to her room when he explained.

"No, repairing books often gets neglected and books languish here for years." Basil took in the room once again, something in him tugging at the sight of so many hurting books.

"I don't even like books, and this just looks sad." Meg brushed her hands on the front of her dress, facing the room. "Show me what to do, and I'll set to work. Someone obviously needs to take this place in hand."

With her brisk tone and confident stance, Basil had a feeling this room would look decidedly better by nightfall than it did now. Not only that, but Meg seemed happier than she had from the moment he'd brought her to the Fae Realm. That happiness sparkled in her eyes and curved her bow-shaped mouth into something that had him staring, his heart thumping harder.

Meg raised her eyebrows, giving him a look.

Right. Repairing books. That was what he was supposed to be thinking about.

He dug into one of the inner pockets of his coat, pulling out two bookbinding needles and a spool of thread.

Meg took a seat in the nearest chair, tugging a book toward her. "How much stuff do you have in those pockets of yours? You always seem to have exactly what we need."

Basil set the items on the table, then opened his coat to show her the four large pockets on the inside. "The top two pockets on each side store whatever items I put into them, no matter how big or heavy. The bottom two pockets are like the cupboards and wardrobes in the cottage. They will pull items from elsewhere if I need something other than what I normally carry with me."

"Sounds very handy." She picked up one of the book-binding needles, gripping it with a steady hand as if it felt comfortable and familiar to her.

"It is." Basil sank into the seat across from her. He showed her how to sew the binding of a book, something she took to with alacrity. It took her a little longer to figure out how to call on the Library to duplicate pages that had been damaged or even duplicate whole books into a previously blank one, but she figured it out, and was soon chatting to the Library just as she did the House.

For its part, the Library responded helpfully once Meg started talking to it, and it eased something inside Basil's chest to see Meg and the Library building a rapport.

"Basil!" Lysander's voice rang so loudly Meg jumped, and Basil nearly stabbed himself with his book repair needle.

Meg whirled around, gaping, as Lysander strode into the room, Hermia clutching his arm as if she refused to let them be parted even for a moment.

Lysander was grinning broadly, glancing between Basil and Meg. "I heard you really did it! You stole yourself a bride! I didn't think you had it in you!"

Even as Lysander pounded him on the back, Basil staggered to his feet, flicking an apologetic glance in Meg's direction. "Lysander, Hermia. This is my wife, Meg. Meg, meet Lysander and Hermia, two of my fellow assistant librarians."

Meg's eyes widened, her mouth forming an O, probably realizing that she was finally meeting half of the Foolish Four. She scrambled to her feet, giving a small wave to them as if not sure what to do.

Hermia let go of her death grip on Lysander's arm and,

instead, clutched Meg's upper arms. "Ah, fair Meg. It is a pleasure to meet you."

Meg glanced past Hermia to meet Basil's gaze, forehead scrunching as if she were at a loss for how to respond. Basil shrugged. He rarely knew how to respond to them either.

"Hermia!" Demetrius stalked around the corner, his blond hair perfectly in place. His fists were clenched, and he looked about ready to start a brawl right there in the Great Library. "Do you so disrespect your father and mine that you would stand there with that…that…"

"I love Lysander!" Hermia let go of Meg's arms and returned to Lysander's side. "Can you speak so true when you claim to love me, Demetrius? Nay, it is your pride talking, not your heart, when you claim such."

Meg eased closer to Basil and whispered, "What is going on?"

"A mess," Basil murmured in return, also keeping his voice too low for the others to hear. "These *are* the Foolish Four, as Buddy calls them."

"Demetrius!" The shriek was so loud, so piercing, that it sent all the nearby bookwyrms scurrying into the shelves to hide.

Helena charged into the room, her blonde curls gleaming.

Demetrius's face blanched and, with a final glare at Hermia and Lysander, he hurried around the end of another set of shelves, Helena racing after him still wailing his name.

Lysander and Hermia made a break in the other direction, leaving Basil and Meg's corner quiet once again.

Meg let out a whoosh of a breath. "Screeching tomcats, now I understand why Buddy calls them the Foolish Four."

"They weren't always this bad." Basil rubbed at the back of his neck. "We all were close friends, until they started falling in love with each other. Even then, it wasn't that bad since they had fallen in love in pairs. Hermia and Lysander.

Helena and Demetrius. But then Hermia's father and Demetrius's father took it in their heads to arrange a marriage between their children, and Demetrius, ever the dutiful son, decided he was in love with Hermia instead of Helena. And it has been a mess ever since."

"Arranged a marriage? I thought participating in that Revel thing in the Tanglewood or snatching a bride were the only ways for a fae to get a mate." Meg returned to her seat and took up her needle again.

"No, there are other ways, like fated mates or bargains or arranged marriages, though that is mostly in the nobility." As he sat, Basil gestured in the direction that Hermia and Lysander had gone. He would have to join them soon, as much as he enjoyed lingering here with Meg. "Those four are all from noble families, working at the Great Library as a rite of passage before they take their places in the court of our king."

As Meg opened her mouth to respond, Master Domitius marched into the room, his black coat making him look like a crow about to pounce on carrion. "I heard a commotion, and what do I find? Here you are, Basil, lazing around with your new bride while there are people waiting to be served."

Jaw knotting, Basil hopped to his feet, giving a small bob of his head. He shouldn't have lingered back here so long. "Yes, sir. I'll see to them, sir."

"Good." With another glower first at Basil, then at Meg, the master librarian spun on his heel and stalked off.

Meg stood, crossing her arms. "What's his problem?"

"He doesn't think a lowly librarian like me from a back-water like Bog's End should have been promoted to the Great Library, even as an assistant librarian." Basil grimaced, unable to meet Meg's gaze. He didn't want to see her pity.

"In other words, you're the fae version of me. Good ol' peasant stock." Instead of pity, a smile tugged at Meg's face.

"Pretty much." Basil shrugged, then waved to the piles of books in need of repair. "You can stay here, if you want. I'll check in with you when I can."

Meg glanced around, then pushed away from the table. "If you don't mind, I think I'll stick with you. I can always come back here for a while later."

She wanted to stay with him. Why did that fill his chest with such warmth? He couldn't help but grin. "I don't mind at all."

Meg trotted along at his side, and it felt right having her there.

In the atrium, a group of male goblins waited beneath the large tree. The goblins all had animalistic features, ears, and tails. One male possessed a massive mane and tawny tail. Another had fox ears and a black, dog-like nose. But most striking was the one with large donkey ears and a gray donkey's tail.

Now Basil understood Domitius's grumpy mood. There was a level of snobbery in the Fae Realm toward goblins, brownies, nymphs, and the like, especially among those like Domitius.

At least Basil knew Meg wouldn't hold those prejudices. If anything, he had a feeling she would find this particular group rather endearing. He whispered, "You're going to like these fae."

Ignoring her raised eyebrows, Basil hurried forward. "Bottom, Quince, what brings you to the Library?"

The fox-faced goblin, Peter Quince, cleared his throat. "We're going to perform a play for good King Theseus's wedding and would like a script."

The donkey-eared goblin, Nick Bottom, pressed forward. "Something tragic! Something glorious! Something to bring the audience to the highest of heights, and the lowest of lows!"

"Isn't King Theseus getting married in two days?" Meg glanced around at the group.

"But of course! That's why we are here. We must practice night and day until our grand performance." Bottom flourished his hands in a grand gesture. Then, he halted, blinked, and swung toward Meg. "Who are you?"

Basil lightly rested his hand on the small of her back. He probably shouldn't have felt so satisfied when she didn't pull away. "This is my wife, Meg. Meg, this is Nick Bottom, Peter Quince, and their acting troupe. They are goblin tradesmen who moved here to the Court of Knowledge to train to become actors."

Quince stepped forward, but Bottom shoved past him, grasped Meg's hand, and pumped it enthusiastically. "A pleasure to meet you. A pure pleasure."

Meg smiled. "Good to meet you. All of you."

"You said you are in need of a script?" Basil's mouth quirked. He was glad Meg was taking Bottom and this troupe in stride.

"Yes, yes, of course. We wish to perform a wondrous play to thank King Theseus for his generosity in hosting us while we train in our art." Bottom released Meg's hand, turning back to Basil. "Lead the way, my good fellow."

Still keeping a hand against Meg's lower back, Basil gently steered her toward one of the wings of the Library. Bottom, Quince, and the rest of the acting troupe fell in behind them, Bottom still nattering about his grandiose plans for this play.

After winding between rows upon rows of shelves, they stepped through a columned doorway into a square space surrounded by books and draped with flowering vines. A few cushioned chairs clustered near each of the room's three fireplaces while each of the six tall windows had a window seat to provide plenty of cozy reading nooks here in one of the fiction sections of the Library.

Basil strode right toward the section of shelves containing plays. "Library, please find the script of *Pyramus and Thisbe.*"

One of the vines draping down from the ceiling tapped along one of the lower shelves until it plucked the book it was seeking. The vine held the book out to Basil.

Holding the book in one hand, Basil reached into one of the pockets of his librarian coat and pulled out a small notebook. Instead of a hard, leather-bound cover, this was just a bunch of blank papers sewn together at the spine.

Placing the blank book on top of the book containing the play, Basil tugged on the Library's magic, asking it to duplicate the play onto the blank pages. A faint glow surrounded both books, and the presence of the Library around them grew heavier, more tangible.

Words shimmered into appearance on the blank paper cover. After a moment, the glow faded, and Basil held out the book.

When Bottom and Quince didn't step forward to claim the copy, Meg took it instead. With a smile, she handed it to the lion-maned goblin, who beamed.

Basil settled into a rhythm, duplicating the books, handing the copies to Meg, and she passed them out to the members of the acting troupe. She kept Basil updated on how many copies he still needed so that he didn't have to count the empty-handed members himself.

When he handed over the last play, he had to blink several times to bring the rest of the Library into focus.

Meg and the entire acting troupe stared at him, as if waiting for him to give some signal to dismiss them. "I believe this play should do nicely for you."

Quince bobbed into something between an enthusiastic nod and a bow. "Thank you, Librarian Basil."

Quince turned and walked toward the Library's exit, Bottom and the rest of the troupe gathering at his heels. As he walked, he opened to the first page and started reading through the list of characters, assigning them to members of the troupe as he went.

The last thing Basil heard before they disappeared around the far shelves was Bottom volunteering for each part in turn, including the role of lion that Quince had, of course, assigned to the goblin with the lion's mane and tail.

Meg shook her head and glanced to Basil. "Let me guess. They are terrible actors."

"So terrible it's hilarious." Basil shrugged, not sure what to do with his hands now that he was finished copying the play. *"Pyramus and Thisbe* is a tragic romance. Nothing too deep, and a bit of overwrought acting won't entirely ruin it."

"Do you really think a love story where everyone dies is the right choice to celebrate a wedding?" Meg raised her eyebrows.

He opened his mouth, hesitated, then grimaced. He really should have thought to ask Meg's opinion in the first place. Too late now. "I didn't think of that. Probably not my best choice. But, to be honest, I'm not sure that troupe could pull off a happy story."

"Guess that's true." After a moment, the smile faded from Meg's face, and she stared off into space as if she wasn't seeing the Library around them.

"Is something wrong?" Basil stopped resisting and reached for her hand. Her fingers were tiny but calloused and rough.

Instead of tugging away as he feared, she swayed closer, as if tempted to lean into him. He wanted to tell her that he would be all right if she did just that. But the words stuck in his throat.

After a moment, Meg shook herself and stepped back. "I'm fine. Just thinking about something else we'll have to talk about tonight."

"All right." He wasn't going to press her.

As she tugged her hand free from his, he didn't resist, even if his fingers felt cold and empty afterwards.

"I'm just…" Meg glanced away from him, already walking toward the door. "I'm going to work on repairing books for a while."

He watched her leave, staring at the empty doorway long after she had disappeared.

Strange how much she was coming to mean to him, even after only two days. What would it be like to spend a lifetime with her? Would it turn into something rich and deep, like the love his parents had shared?

It all depended on how well their conversation went tonight. It wasn't going to be easy, confessing that he had snatched her, only to throw her into the deadly Midsummer Night.

# CHAPTER 10

*M*eg eased the needle through the binding, the thick thread rubbing against her fingers in a soothing sensation. A needle. Thread. Familiar things in this unfamiliar place. She couldn't read. She couldn't do much when it came to helping Basil find information in the Library. But she could sew.

Perhaps that was why thoughts of her family ached so deeply today. Were they all right? Had Cullen harmed them? How was Meg supposed to help them now?

She couldn't dwell on her worries for them now. Tonight, she would tell Basil everything. She would trust that he would figure out a solution with that information-stuffed brain of his.

Until then, she relaxed into the rhythm of hard work. She felt at home with the gritty feel of dust coating her fingers and the grime of sweat against her skin after her efforts to organize the piles of books waiting to be mended.

"This looks much better than this morning."

Meg glanced up to find Basil standing in the doorway, his

gaze sweeping over the piles that she had sorted into neat stacks based on how much repair the books needed. She hadn't gotten through all of the spilling mounds of books, but she had managed a good start. In between sorting, she had taken breaks to repair books and now had a neat stack at the end of the table of books that were ready to be returned to the Library's shelves.

Basil strode into the room, his gaze focusing on her. He flashed a smile that was almost tentative, as if he wasn't sure what he was supposed to say after she had left so abruptly earlier. "Thanks for doing such a good job in here today."

Her heart twisted, and she had to drop her gaze to the table. She had been rude earlier. But with worries for her family swirling through her head, she'd needed time to think, and it had taken the quiet solitude to come to grips with her decision to trust Basil with her family.

"Thanks. I think this is my favorite room in the Library." Meg smiled, hoping something about her regret for walking away earlier came through in her voice and expression.

"And all the librarians will appreciate it if this mess is cleaned up. Head Librarian Marco's wife occasionally comes in and helps out in here, but she has been busy lately helping her and Marco's daughters with their young children." Basil strode across the room until he was within arm's reach. He scratched at the back of his neck, not meeting Meg's gaze. "My shift is almost over, so I thought I'd check on how you were doing. Sorry I didn't have a chance earlier. The afternoon turned busy."

She opened her mouth, not even sure what she planned to say.

A trilling shriek filled the library, coming from somewhere outside of the wing where Meg and Basil stood. The sound was joined by more screeching and hissing and growling.

Basil stiffened, his eyes widening. He grabbed Meg's hand and broke into a run toward the sound, dragging her with him.

After a few stumbling steps, Meg lengthened her stride to keep pace. "What's going on?"

"The bookwyrms are alerting us to an attack. A monster must have gotten through a thin spot." As he ran, Basil plunged a hand into an inner pocket, withdrawing a long, hardwood club about two feet long.

"A what came through what?" Meg stumbled, torn between digging in her heels and keeping up with Basil.

"Sorry, I'll explain later." Basil remained focused ahead, gripping the club as if prepared to use it.

If a monster was in the Library, running pell-mell toward it didn't sound like the smartest plan to Meg. But what did she know? This was her first monster attack.

But she had fought off her fair share of pests trying to eat the chickens or steal the crops.

As they neared the screeching, Basil slowed down, pressing his back to one set of shelves.

Meg eased into place beside him, tugging her hand free of his. If they were going into battle, she wanted both hands free to fight.

Fight with what weapon, she didn't know. Basil, at least, had his club. After a moment, she located a particularly large, hardcover book on the shelf next to her. Plucking it out, she gripped it with both hands.

Basil leaned around the edge of the shelves, and Meg stood on tiptoe to peek over his shoulder.

In the gloom of a corner formed by the back wall and two sets of shelves, a hulking, chittering form crouched on what seemed like far too many black, hairy legs.

Murdering muskrats. That was a spider. A whacking giant spider the same size as Buddy. And, scuttling in the shadows beneath its belly, more, chicken-sized spiders. Baby spiders, though that seemed too tame a word for the monstrosities.

Around them, even Meg could sense the way the Library shuddered and groaned, as if in both pain and anger. The shelves around the spiders closed over the books they contained, shuffling farther away from the spiders.

Ten bookwyrms lined up across the opening to the corner. Their leathery ruffs puffed to make them appear bigger as they hissed and growled and screeched at the spiders. When one of the smaller spiders scurried too close to one of the bookwyrms, the bookwyrm lashed forward, catching the spider in its teeth and shaking it vigorously, like a stray dog that had caught a rabbit.

Meg might get to like those little slithering biters.

With a clicking sound, three of the smaller spiders rushed toward the bookwyrm chomping on the first spider. With a yelp, the bookwyrm dropped the spider and lurched back out of the spiders' reach.

Basil tightened his grip on his club. "Stay here. Other librarians will be here soon, but I can't wait. I need to help the bookwyrms hold the spiders back. If the spiders get out into the rest of the Library, they'll wreak havoc, and we'll be here all night trying to kill them off."

Meg tightened her grip on the sturdy book. "I'm not staying behind. You need someone to watch your back."

Jaw working, Basil glanced at her, then gave a sharp nod. "Try not to let them bite you. If one does, tell me."

Swallowing, Meg shifted her stance. This wasn't like going into battle against a raccoon or two. These were monstrous spiders unlike anything she had faced before. And, instead of a trusty shovel or sharp hoe, all she had was a book.

Basil faced forward again, his muscles tensed and ready, his eyes hard and focused.

This was a different side of Basil, one she hadn't seen before. Right at first, she'd dismissed him as nothing but a mild-mannered librarian. She might have even been harboring disappointment that he wasn't a lordly warrior fae like the ones in the stories.

But that impression of him hadn't been correct either, not entirely. He wasn't a warrior, who chose to make a living out of fighting. Yet, he was willing to take up a weapon and fight to protect the things that were important to him, such as the Great Library.

If he was willing to fight this hard to protect the Library, then surely he would be willing to fight just as hard for a wife. For her family.

Another group of spiders charged toward the book-wyrms. A dark green bookwyrm threw itself backward, hissing and snarling.

Without so much as a battle cry or warning, Basil charged, gripping his club. He joined the line of bookwyrms and swung his club, smashing one of the smaller spiders to a squishy, yellow-green goo on the floor.

The massive spider gave a screech and batted at Basil with one of its legs. Basil knocked the leg aside with his club.

Branches from the nearby Library shelves struck at the giant spider. Few hits landed as the spider scuttled out of the Library's way.

The smaller spiders rushed toward Basil, but he was too busy with the large spider to deal with many of the smaller critters.

Meg dashed into the fray. One of the spiders had gotten past the bookwyrms and was poised with its clicking mandibles inches from Basil's leg.

She kicked it before it had a chance to bite Basil. Green goo burst across her boot as the spider hurtled backwards before thunking into the solid wood of the closed-over shelves, leaving a viscous smear on the wood.

Several of the bookwyrms darted forward, gripping smaller spiders in their teeth and shaking them viciously.

A spider launched itself over them, and Meg swatted it to the ground with the book before she stomped on it, thankful for her sturdy, knee-high boots.

Swat. Stomp. Swat. Stomp. Meg didn't let herself think about all the spattering spider guts and dripping poison. She didn't even register when other fae librarians arrived, until suddenly the blonde-haired Helena appeared at her side, swinging a club like Basil's and shrieking in an octave Meg hadn't thought a fae or human could reach.

Moments later, Hermia and Lysander bolted past, also swinging clubs, as they joined Basil in pressing the giant spider farther back into the corner. Demetrius smashed at the smaller spiders. He might claim he currently loved Hermia, but in that moment, he was at Helena's side, protecting her.

Meg swatted one last spider with a book, stomping it into mush beneath her foot.

With the gargantuan spider backed into a corner, unable to skitter away, no fewer than ten branches detached from the wall and surrounding shelves. Viciously, the Library battered the giant spider.

The spider shrieked, curling in on itself. It darted, trying to make a break away from the Library's fury, but Basil and the other assistant librarians blocked its advance.

The presence of the Library grew so heavy, so angry, that Meg struggled to breathe. She had to grip one of the Library shelves to stay upright under the weight of the living building pressing around her.

With a thunderclap of angry wood and earth, the Library battered the spider until it was beyond dead and nothing but a pulped smear on the moss floor.

The wooden shelves gave a groan, and the moss floor rose up beneath Meg's feet. The Library swallowed the bodies of the smashed, smaller spiders. Like a wave along the seashore, the moss rolled forward, lifting Basil and the others, before it engulfed the remains of the giant spider.

When the Library stilled, no sign of the spiders remained. A calm silence reigned once again, the Library peaceful. The shelves around them were swept clean of gore, though the bookwyrms and librarians were spattered with the muck of the monster battle.

Meg pushed away from the shelves as they began to shift, revealing their rows upon rows of books once again. When she swiped at the hair falling across her face, her fingers came away sticky with a yellow-green substance.

Ick. She grimaced and swiped her fingers on a semi-clean patch on her skirt. The House was going to have a fit when she and Basil arrived home.

Basil glanced around, then pushed past a kissing Hermia and Lysander, a glowering Demetrius, and a clinging, shaking Helena to return to Meg's side. He swiped at her forehead, his fingers coming away covered with even more goop. "Are you all right?"

For some reason, Meg found herself grinning, her knees a little weak. He, too, was spattered with blotches of yellow-green goo. His green coat hid most of its damage, but his gray shirt was rumpled and open, giving her a very nice view of his chest.

If he expected her to be all faint and swooning at the icki-ness of battle, then he would be disappointed.

She smirked, reaching out to flick some of the spider guts from his shoulder. "I'm a farmgirl. I've killed pests and butchered animals. This is hardly the grossest thing I've ever done. Though, the Library eating the bodies afterwards was pretty disgusting. I thought you said the Library didn't eat things."

"It doesn't eat people or living things. But dead monsters are just food, like any decomposing body in a forest." Basil's gaze dropped to the book she held in her hand, his expression twisting into gaping dismay. "What have you done to that book?"

Meg hefted the trusty hardcover she had wielded as a weapon. One cover was torn and smeared with spider guts. More goop coated the edges of the pages. She shrugged. "I had to use something against the spiders."

"But...the book...You got spider guts all over it!" Basil sputtered, such a depth of utter horror in his voice that Meg had to swallow back a laugh.

"It's fine. I'll fix it tomorrow." Meg swiped the book against her bodice, cleaning off the cover and pages as best she could. It remained stained and sticky.

As if the Library had just realized what she held, a branch detached from the nearby shelf and plucked the book from her hands. A sense of supreme huffiness filled the space before the Library shoved the book into Basil's hands, as if ordering him to fix the mess. As the branch returned to the bookshelves, it flicked Meg's shoulder hard enough to sting.

"Ow!" Meg rubbed the spot, glaring at the shelves. "What was that for? I just saved your ever-precious books from those whacking big critters, and this is the thanks I get?"

A muffled sound came from Basil. A moment later, a deep chuckle rumbled in his chest, and he bent, resting his hands on his knees as he laughed.

Meg tried to fight her own laughter, but she couldn't help it. The Library's exasperation was just too funny.

Her laugh joined Basil's, filling the corner of the Library. Once she started, she couldn't stop, giving in to the joy of laughing again after far too long.

## CHAPTER 11

When Basil stumbled through the Anywhere Door into the House, his bones ached with weariness. His skin crawled with the need to wash off the gritty, sticky remnants of spiders. All he wanted to do was wash in the grotto, then collapse into bed, even though he had promised Meg they would talk tonight.

Beside him, Meg's gore-smeared face and tousled hair gave her a weary, disheveled appearance. She slumped against the Door to shut it behind them.

Around them, the whole House gave a start, then a horrified kind of shudder.

Buddy poked his head over the half door to his stall. "What's got the House—oh, that explains it. You two are a mess."

"It was a rough day. Spiders." Basil rubbed a hand across his face, knocking flakes of dried spider guts from his skin.

The House gave the impression of a shriek—though it wasn't audible. Then the Anywhere Door flung open, knocking Meg into Basil's chest. Through the open doorway, the bathing grotto wafted steam into the room.

Basil cleared his throat and steadied Meg. "Would you like to clean up first?"

She nodded, rushing into the grotto with much more eagerness than she had on her first day there.

While Meg washed, Basil eased out of his librarian coat, scowling at the stains. The House would have to work hard to get it cleaned up before tomorrow.

"Meg seems to have handled her first monster attack well." Buddy trotted from his stall, inspecting Basil as if checking for any injuries. "That's a good sign, considering you still haven't told her about Midsummer Night."

Basil inspected the monster blood dried on his hands. "Yes, she waded into the fight without any hesitation."

He had been disappointed, yesterday, when she had told him she couldn't read. But, perhaps, a well-learned human who could read and write wasn't the wife he'd needed. Meg, with her willingness to tackle the book repair room and her unflinching bravery in the face of a giant spider, had proved herself far better than the mythical dream girl he'd hoped for.

He couldn't help but grin as he glanced up to Buddy. "Though, I might have to get her a weapon. She destroyed a book using it on the spiders."

"Shocking."

"I know. I couldn't believe anyone would treat a book with such disrespect." Basil struggled to keep a straight face.

Buddy snorted. "I will have to ask Meg to describe the look on your face. I'm sure it was priceless."

Basil didn't even bother to respond.

When Meg reappeared, her blonde hair was wet, and she wore a clean dress similar to the one she had been wearing before. She gestured behind her. "It's all yours."

Basil rushed through bathing, thankful to scrub away all the monster guts. By the time he finished, the House had provided a clean set of clothes, though his librarian coat was still missing.

At least being clean had refreshed him so that he felt more prepared for that long conversation he needed to have with Meg.

He left the collar of his shirt open, rolling up his sleeves to just below his elbows as he strolled from the grotto back to the main room of the House.

There, he found Meg transferring food from the cupboard onto an already overflowing tray. She glanced up, something in her gaze warming at the sight of him. "I thought I'd ask the cupboard for supper while I was waiting. It decided to be generous tonight."

"Yes, it did." Glancing from the tray to Meg, Basil drew in a deep breath and gathered his courage. "Why don't we eat in the glade?"

"A picnic? Sure, why not." Meg picked up the tray and took a step toward the Anywhere Door.

One of the kitchen cupboards opened and spat out a wad of red-and-white checked fabric, hitting Meg in the chest.

Basil reached to steady Meg before she dropped the tray. The House was definitely taking on more of a personality since he'd brought Meg home.

And there he was, calling the cottage *House* the way Meg had been.

Meg juggled the tablecloth and tray. "Reckon the House likes the idea of a picnic also."

Basil took the tray from her, then waited as she opened the Anywhere Door for the two of them.

The Door opened to a quiet forest glade, carpeted by clover and a variety of other flowers in all colors from red to yellow to white. Willows with their graceful branches trailing to the ground surrounded the clearing while a gurgling, clear stream meandered between the willows.

"This is lovely." Meg peered over his shoulder. "Is it safe? Something that pretty has to be dangerous."

"The magic that links it to the Door encloses this tiny section of forest so that as long as we are inside, the only way in or out is through our Door." Basil stepped through the doorway.

On the glade side, the Door was formed of a stone arch and thick bark door set beneath one of the willows. A floral, sweet aroma hung heavy in the glade, kept from being too stifling thanks to other scents of clear water and wet earth.

Basil set the tray on one of the large, smooth rocks that broke through the otherwise solid carpet of moss, clover, and flowers. "Other Doors in our Court connect to this place as well, since I'm not high ranking enough to have a protected glade all to myself. If someone else wants to use it, the Door will alert us, and we can either leave or opt to share."

"Huh." Meg stepped into the glade, turning in a circle. Her eyebrows scrunched. "There's no birdsong."

"As I said, nothing can get in or out." Basil suppressed a shudder. "Believe me, you don't want birds getting in. Most are rather deadly."

"Ah." Meg gestured to the clearing with one hand, still gripping the tablecloth bundle with her other arm. "If the only way in or out is through the Door, does that mean there's nothing on the other side of these willows?"

"Not exactly." Basil took the tablecloth from her and spread it on the ground. "This is just a small section of forest, and there probably is a way to stumble out of the protected glade if you aren't careful. Not something you want to do, unless you want to find yourself at the mercy of sprites like Puck or other fae like him. But, most likely, the protections would just gently turn you around so that you would find yourself back here no matter which direction you walk."

Meg gave a shudder, then plopped onto the tablecloth.

"Staying right here sounds fine by me."

Sitting here in the glade, with her, held a strange tension between peace and awkwardness. This was what he'd always wanted to enjoy with a mate. Picnics in the glade. Laughter. A deeper companionship.

Yet, Meg was still mostly a stranger, giving this moment a taut edge instead of relaxed enjoyment.

The evening sunlight streamed shafts of orange-gold light between the willow branches, painting brighter highlights in Meg's blonde hair. Her brown eyes sparkled, her round face holding a glow. She had a spark, a bright personality.

His mouth went dry, his heart beating harder.

Meg reached for the plate of bright orange vegetables, eyed them for a moment, shrugged, then dug in. "So, you were going to explain about monsters and thin spots and stuff."

Basil shook off the twisting in his chest and claimed one of the pieces of bread. This was it. Either she would take this in stride, or she would hate him for bringing her here to this dangerous place. "The Fae Realm overlaps your Human Realm in places, and where the realms meet, there are thin spots in the barrier where people can cross."

Meg stuffed a large bite into her mouth and chewed with her mouth open. "Like the faerie circle where you found me."

"Exactly. Here in the Fae Realm, we have the same thing, but with the Realm of Monsters." Basil nibbled at the toast. He was hungry, even if his stomach twisted as he waited for Meg's reaction. "The barrier between the realms keeps the monsters out, for the most part. But there are still thin spots, and monsters can get through. At the more magical times in our Realm, the barrier wears even thinner, such as on Midsummer Night. Violence and evil deeds can also make the barrier between realms wear thin. I've heard that in some places, like the Court of Sand, the barriers between Human,

Fae, and Monster Realms are so thin that sometimes monsters get all the way into the Human Realm."

"Sounds dreadful." Meg gave a shudder and reached for the rest of the bread.

"It is." Buddy's voice came from the now open Door a moment before he stuck his head through the doorway. The rest of him followed a moment later. His brown, sleek body filled the glade. "There is a herd of talking horses who moved into the Human Realm near a place connected to the Court of Sand. They are constantly having to fight monsters in both the Fae and Human Realms."

"I'm glad I ended up in this Court." Meg shoveled a large bite of the pink bread into her mouth.

"Don't be too comforted. This Court has its own challenges." Buddy snorted, his eyes swiveling in an approximation of an eyeroll. "Namely, the next-door neighbors."

"I know how that goes." Meg shivered again, her mouth twisting as if she was suddenly queasy.

Basil chewed and swallowed. "You remember Puck? He's the lackey of King Oberon, who rules the Court of Revels with his wife Queen Titania. They have an interesting relationship. Sometimes, they are utterly in love. Other times, they are so at odds that they come close to killing each other. When that happens, the animosity and hatred in that Court wears the barrier to the Realm of Monsters thin."

Meg gave a shudder and set aside her now empty plate. "Puck was horrible enough."

Basil shook his head, his own shudder starting in his back. "Oberon and Titania are worse. Most of the cruelest tales you've heard about the Fae Realm—fae snatching humans to torture them as entertainment, feeding humans faerie fruit, seducing humans for twisted pleasures—are all caused by the Court of Revels. We fae are a wild, unbridled lot, but the Court of Revels is the wildest, even when at its best. When Oberon and Titania really go at it, they plunge all of the surrounding Courts, including the Court of Knowledge, into chaos. And all signs are pointing toward that happening again here shortly."

"And, because it is Midsummer, the chaos will be even worse. But do they care about that? No." Buddy gave that snort again before he went back to munching the foliage.

"At least Midsummer Night is the shortest night of the year." Meg picked up another plate of food and dug in.

Basil set aside his plate, unable to finish. "Time doesn't work the same way in the Fae Realm as it does in your world." He only knew that since he had researched how time moved in the various realms for a king of the Court of Stone a while ago. "As the Court of Knowledge is in the section of the Fae Realm that experiences perpetual summer, our most magical time is Midsummer, especially Midsummer Night. Thus, Midsummer is both our longest day and our longest night."

"That makes no sense." Meg paused in shoveling food into her mouth long enough to give Basil an exasperated look.

"If that's not enough, Midsummer doesn't come around on a regular basis." Buddy spoke around a mouthful of grass and clover, his tail swishing back and forth. "Sometimes, during particularly magical times, Midsummer shows up three months apart. Other times, it takes ages between Midsummers."

"This whole Fae Realm is crazier than a sugared-up raccoon, you know that?" Meg scrubbed her fingers on the ends of her swirling skirt.

"True. But you are finding us at a bad time." Buddy trotted a few steps closer to Meg, though he never fully lifted his head from the clover. "The Court of Revels wasn't always this bad. It was downright nice before the Deplorable Duo took over."

"You really need to stop giving everyone nicknames." Basil glared, leaning back on his hands.

Meg leaned her elbows on her knees. "Do I even want to know what nickname you've given me?"

"Nope." Buddy shook his mane, eyeing Basil. "You have to admit, Deplorable Duo fits them rather well."

"Yes, though don't let King Oberon or Queen Titania catch you saying that." Basil glanced around the glade. Even though it was protected, it never hurt to be too careful where the rulers of the Court of Revels were concerned.

Meg shifted, then leaned against one of the moss-covered rocks that dotted the glade. "You said that the Court of Revels wasn't always as bad as it is now. What did you mean?"

"The previous king was *much* more sensible, that's what." Buddy bobbed his head decisively. "It made life better all around."

"How would you know? You weren't even born then." Basil resisted the urge to roll his eyes.

Buddy shook one front hoof in Basil's direction. "No, but we talking equines remember our history. A lesson you fae should learn. Then the Court of Revels wouldn't have forgotten its purpose."

"There's a purpose to revelry?" Meg eyed him, as if already doubting whatever response he would give.

Basil took a moment to think through his response. "Revelry isn't just the debauched pursuit of mindless, excessive—and often cruel—pleasures as King Oberon and Titania have turned it into. It is supposed to be a place of art. No matter how seemingly frivolous, art can give a laugh, a light, a spark of pleasure that relieves sorrow and uplifts the soul. It can tell truths and reach hearts better than dry, pedantic tomes. That's the true purpose of the Court of Revels."

"I see." Meg shrugged. "You're rather passionate about the

topic."

Basil plucked a clover and twirled it in his fingers. "It's a big debate in the Court of Knowledge."

Buddy's snort was so loud that Basil jumped, then shook himself, taking Buddy's cue to stop talking before he turned this discussion into a lecture on the worth of art.

"So, anyway, that's what I had to explain to you." Basil stared down at the clover pinched in his fingers. "Mid-summer Night is tomorrow night, and it will probably be a bad one with a lot of monsters that will make that spider look tame."

Perhaps snatching a mate *right* before the most dangerous season here in the Court of Knowledge wasn't his best plan.

Meg drew in a deep breath, releasing it with a shudder. "All right. Monsters. Got it. Will I at least get a weapon tomorrow night?"

"Yes, of course. I'll pull one out of my coat for you just as soon as the House finishes cleaning it." Basil sagged as all the twisting tension left his chest. That had gone far better than he'd feared.

"Not sure why the House is bothering." Meg sat up, adjusting her sitting position. "Our clothes are just going to get all mucked up again tomorrow."

"At least we have a magical House doing all the cleaning for us." Basil smiled, even if it felt a touch strained.

"All that scrubbing." She gave an exaggerated shiver.

Scrubbing she must have done, back in the Human Realm.

It was time Basil prodded Meg to talk about herself. "Um, well…" He scratched the back of his neck. "There was a question I was supposed to ask…"

Buddy raised his head, grass sticking out of the corners of his mouth. "He wants to ask why you ran away from home hoping to get snatched by the fae."

"Buddy!" Basil growled between clenched teeth. "You aren't helping."

"You need all the help you can get." Buddy flicked his tail, its ends stinging Basil's hand.

Across the tablecloth, Meg stared at her hands. Her back wasn't stiff like she was angry. Nor was her mouth hanging open in shock. After a moment, she peeked up at Basil. "No, it's all right. You ought to know."

With a deep breath, she started her story of the drought, her parents' deaths, the man named Cullen planning to sell her, her desperate choice to run away and hope to earn enough to rescue her family.

Basil worked to keep his expression neutral. When the heat building inside his chest grew too much, he pushed to his feet and paced, gripping his hands behind his back.

This was all far more than he had bargained for when he'd decided to snatch a bride from the Human Realm. For some reason, he hadn't expected her to come with baggage and a family.

But, there wasn't much of a choice, in the end. Meg was his mate. That meant her problems were his problems.

He knew exactly what he'd have to do.

As she finished spilling her story to Basil, Meg held her breath. What would he think of her? How would he react?

So far, his angular face had remained so carefully stoic that it twisted something inside her. She wasn't even sure how to hope, or what to hope for. Sure, Basil had all his needs provided for him due to being a part of the Court of Knowledge. But he wasn't some rich fae lord like she had been imagining when she had run into the forest. He didn't seem to have the money to pay off Cullen.

Finally, Basil turned toward her, his hands still clasped behind his back. "We'll have to snatch your siblings and take them here to live with us."

Meg's chest tightened, and her breath strangled into a lump at the back of her throat. She could take her family here? That was allowed?

Basil rushed on, his words coming faster and faster as if he was worried about her reaction. "It won't be as easy for them as it was for you, since they won't have the marriage binding to protect them. But we can make it work. I'm sure the House will expand enough to hold them, and Head Librarian Marco will understand why I need more of a share of the Court's magical resources to support your family."

She pressed her hands over her mouth, tears heating the corners of her eyes. When she'd run, she had thought her best option would be to trade herself for a fae lord's wealth, sacrificing to buy her family a better life in their drought-ravaged land.

But such a future would always tear apart what was left of her family. She would be stuck in the Fae Realm while her siblings remained in the human world.

Instead, Basil was giving her a way to keep her family together. She could take her brother and sisters out of their desperate situation entirely. Yes, the Fae Realm was weird and wondrous, beautiful and dangerous. But it would be a far better life for her family here, even with the dangers, than back in their drought-dead village.

Buddy had been right. Here, in this Realm and with Basil, Meg had the opportunity to build a life beyond anything she had ever dreamed.

"Well? What do you think?" Basil's shoulders slumped, his gaze fixed on the now rather crushed clover in his hands instead of on her.

Meg couldn't hold the emotion back any longer. She

jumped to her feet, not even sure how to express everything she was thinking and feeling.

In that moment, if just for his care for her family, she fell in love with him.

Slowly, she stepped closer to him and wrapped her arms around him. He was warm and stiff, and it took her a moment to figure out if she was supposed to hug around his neck or around his waist, and she ended up awkwardly embracing him with one arm above and one arm below.

She had never been this close to a man before. Basil's shirt smelled faintly of the Great Library. A mix of leather and old paper and ink. She also caught a whiff of some other spice. The longer she stood there, leaning into the hard warmth of his chest beneath his soft shirt, the more she relaxed into the comfort his solidness provided.

After yet another long moment, Basil's arms came around her, resting lightly on her back.

That soft touch drained the last of her strength, and she found herself all but slumping into his hold, clinging to him as she pressed her face into his shirt.

Buddy's muffled hoofbeats on the moss and clover clopped closer before his voice came from behind Basil. "Told you that was the right question to ask."

Buddy's tone was so smug that Meg laughed against Basil's shoulder, even as Buddy's hoofbeats moved away, followed by the click of the Door shutting.

Basil's shoulders lifted and fell beneath her as his sigh stirred her hair. "Sorry. Buddy is…"

"He is a dear," Meg murmured against Basil's shirt. She didn't have the willpower to move.

For the first time since her parents' deaths, she was safe. Her sisters and brother would soon be safe. And she didn't have to keep up that prickly guard to protect herself.

"I...uh..." Basil cleared his throat, his hands shifting against her back as if he wasn't sure what to do now.

Drawing the last bit of her strength, Meg pushed away from him, though she didn't step fully out of his arms. "Thank you. For being willing to give my sisters and brother a home. That means so, so much and I..." She couldn't finish, that aching lump filling the back of her throat.

"About that..." Basil eased farther back from her, scratching at his collar. "I know you probably want to fetch them right away, and I agree we need to rescue them as soon as possible. But Midsummer Night this year is going to be deadly. It will be perilous enough for you and me. But as humans without the added protection of a strong binding, your family would be in more peril here than in your world."

"Right." Meg's stomach sank, that brief hope deflating at the reality of his words.

It hurt, having to leave her siblings in continued danger for a few more days. For all they knew, Meg had died in the forest, her body eaten by scavengers and never to be found. Or she had been hauled off by less savory merchants or even Cullen's men. Worry for Meg had to be eating away at them, breaking down their resolve and hope.

What if they ran, as she had told them to, before she got back? What if she returned to find an empty hut?

She straightened her shoulders. Her family was strong. They would survive for a few more days. Surely they wouldn't have been forced to run just yet. "I don't like leaving them back there, but a few more days won't hurt, considering the danger they would be in if we brought them here."

Basil's gaze swiveled away from her as he scrubbed a hand over his face. "That's the thing. Time doesn't move the same way between your world and mine. With the Midsummer ties to your realm so strong right now, I don't think more than a few months—maybe a year or two at the most—will pass in your world by the time we can go back there. But you ought to know the risk, in not bringing them here right away."

Meg clenched her fists, pacing away from him as she processed that. How could she abandon her sisters and brother for months? If longer than a year passed, then her family would flee, and she would never find them.

But how could she bring them here when they were about to face a deluge of monsters?

She spun on her heel to face Basil again. "How much time has already passed?"

He winced. "I don't know. Probably only a few months. I'm sorry, truly. I didn't think. I should have realized you had left a family behind." He ran a hand through his hair, tousling the dark strands even more than they already were. "The traditions make snatching a bride sound so simple. And there you were at the circle, alone. And you never mentioned..." He sighed. "I just didn't think."

Why was it so annoyingly difficult to stay angry with him when he looked so adorable? Tousled hair, liquid brown eyes, chiseled features lacking any hardness of cruelty.

When she exhaled slowly, the tension in her chest eased. "When I ran from home, I never intended to tell whatever fae snatched me about my sisters and brother, thinking to protect them. I just wanted enough faerie gold to buy their protection. I never expected...this." She gestured between her and Basil, then around at the glade. "I didn't think I'd find a home."

His gaze snapped up to hers. Then, a tentative smile crossed his face, deepening the liquid pools of his brown eyes.

Meg found herself giving him a smile in return, surprised by how much she meant that.

## CHAPTER 12

*B*asil's stomach churned as he shrugged into his librarian coat. Outside the cottage, the last, pink rays of the setting sun highlighted all of the homes along the winding street. The white castle on the hill basked in the pink-gold light while the glass-domed top of the Library gleamed.

Midsummer Night. In the Tanglewood and in the Court of Revels, it was a night for frivolity and pleasures. Here in the Court of Knowledge, they braced for the danger.

The clop of hooves and the stamp of feet passed his door. All of the fighting men and women of the Court were out tonight, patrolling the village, the castle, and the borders of the Tanglewood. Hippolyta's swordmaidens were interspersed among the patrols, providing extra protection for a night that looked to be the most chaotic they had experienced in their lifetimes.

Meg stepped from her room, straightening the folds of her skirts. Her boots laced to her knees, also cleaned of the spider guts. Her jaw set, she faced him. "Do you have another club for me? I'd rather go into battle armed this time, and I don't think you or the Library want me using a book."

The House around them gave a shudder, then a hardwood shepherd's staff, complete with the curved top, fell from the ceiling and landed at Meg's feet.

After picking up the staff, she glanced toward the ceiling, her mouth curving into a smile. "Thank you, House. I appreciate your care."

The House gave a satisfied shake.

With Meg smiling, Basil found it hard to tear his eyes away from her. It wasn't just her beauty—her golden hair, sparkling brown eyes, and pert mouth—but the expressions that flashed across her face spoke of her determination to save her siblings and her fearlessness to sass a magical House and an ancient Library. All things that he was coming to love about her.

He'd come close to kissing her several times now. When she smiled at him, he could barely think, much less breathe.

He shook himself. He couldn't afford to be distracted. Not on Midsummer Night.

The door to the outside opened, and Buddy trotted inside. He shook his mane, flicking droplets of something wet onto the wall. "A few more of those spiders raided the village, but they've all been squashed. You'd better head for the Library."

Basil pulled his club from one of his pockets. "Yes. They'll need everyone."

Buddy crossed the room and bumped Meg's shoulder with his nose. "Stay safe. Look after Basil for me."

Meg stepped forward and hugged Buddy's neck. "Stay safe yourself. It won't be easy, defending the House tonight."

Buddy nibbled on her hair and gave a tug, smirking as much as a pony could. "I'll be fine."

With a final pat to Buddy's neck, Meg pulled away and opened the Anywhere Door, revealing the bustling hall.

As she stepped through, Basil halted next to Buddy and lowered his voice. "If something should happen to me tonight, promise me you'll look after Meg?"

Buddy nipped Basil's shoulder, his blunt teeth knocking hard enough to hurt. "Don't talk like that. You'll be fine."

"I know, I know. I'm not going into this all fatalistic." Basil rubbed at the back of his neck, unable to meet Buddy's large brown eyes. "I just need to know that Meg will be all right, if something should happen. Promise me you would look after her and that you would see to it that her siblings are fetched here, if that's what she still wanted?"

"I promise." Buddy's voice rang with a somber tone Basil had never heard from him before.

Good. Buddy understood how serious Basil was about this. No matter what happened, he had to make sure Meg was all right. He had brought her into this mess when he had snatched her from her realm. The least he could do was make sure this realm was the safe haven she had been looking for when she'd run into the forest that night.

With a deep breath, Basil strode through the Anywhere Door and into chaos.

Led by Queen Hippolyta, swordmaidens shouted as they charged across the room, swords and spears drawn, before they launched themselves at a chimera, a monstrous creature with the body of a lion, a goat's head on one end, and a snake's head on the other so that it was hard to tell what was the head and what functioned as the tail. The chimera's goat's head spat a gout of fire at Hippolyta, but she dodged and struck down with her spear, piercing the creature where its head met its neck.

Crab-like creatures with pincers the size of dinner plates scuttled at the edges of the room, chased by fighting men and women of King Theseus's Court as they smashed the crab monsters as quickly as possible. Harpies fluttered around the edges, squawking and flapping and striking at any of the defenders who came too close.

King Theseus stood in the center of the room, sword in hand, as he directed the response to the influx of monsters.

Meg had placed her back against the wall next to the Door. Instead of a mask of fear, her face set in hard lines as she gripped her staff as if prepared to thunk anything that came too close.

When Basil reached her side, she hefted her weapon. "I'm not sure this is going to be enough."

"Probably not. This is the most chaotic Midsummer Night I've ever seen." Basil's chest tightened. The night had only begun, though he didn't say that out loud. "Are you handling this all right?"

She shrugged and gestured with her staff. "These aren't that different from the pests I've had to fend off back home. Sure, they are a little bigger. A little stranger. But those hawk-women are basically chicken hawks. That crazy critter over there is a mix of a nasty billy goat, a snake, and a mountain lion. Sure, it's all mixed up together, but it's still killable."

Perhaps Meg couldn't read. She wasn't at all the mate he'd pictured when he'd set out to snatch a human bride.

But she was a tough, sensible farmgirl who could face the chaos of Midsummer Night without flinching. She wasn't ignorant or unintelligent. No, she was smart in the way that mattered to her. An expert in her particular field, the same way he was in his.

Now wasn't the time to tell her all this. They had to survive the night first.

He grabbed Meg's free hand and tugged her toward the large, double doors that led to the Library. "Come on."

Together, they dodged between the chaos of swordmaidens fighting harpies and King Theseus's nobles smashing crabs. At the doors, Basil had to let go of Meg to use both hands to tug open one of the large doors.

As he and Meg hurried inside the Library, they stepped from one scene of chaos into another. Growls and squeaks filled the air as bookwyrms chased giant rats even bigger than they were. Librarians waved clubs and joined the bookwyrms in chasing the unusually-sized rodents.

Near the tree under the Library's central dome, three of the rats cornered a luminescent yellow bookwyrm. It shrieked as one of the rodents bit the end of its tail.

Basil stepped forward to help the bookwyrm, but he wouldn't be able to get there quickly enough.

With a surprisingly loud war cry and his long white beard looped over his shoulder, Head Librarian Marco raced past, brandishing his club. He struck out at the rodents, sending them flying back, away from the beleaguered bookwyrm.

Steps behind Head Librarian Marco, his wife swooped in, wielding a cast iron frying pan. She picked up the bookwyrm, inspected its bite wound, and cradled the shaking creature close.

"Giant rats. Of course." Meg shrugged and swung her shepherd's staff at a massive rodent that scurried too close.

Master Librarian Domitius marched over to them, scowling. "Basil. You're finally here."

"I came as soon as I could, sir." Basil gritted his teeth. Even now, Domitius couldn't resist a chance to berate him.

Head Librarian Marco appeared next to Domitius, smoothing out his long white beard over his chest. "Don't be so hard on the boy. Basil, at least, had the sense to snatch himself a wife before Midsummer Night. He didn't leave us shorthanded the way many of his fellow assistant librarians did."

As expected, Lysander, Hermia, Demetrius, and Helena

must have all run off to the Revel. Probably some of the other unmated librarians as well, abandoning the Library on its most dangerous night.

Meg raised her shepherd's crook, glaring at Domitius. "Of course Basil didn't leave this Library in danger. He loves this Library. More than you do, I reckon. Otherwise you'd recognize someone else who does."

Domitius's face mottled, reddened. "Why you little human wench! How dare you—"

"Don't say another word." Basil stepped between Meg and Domitius, his grip white-knuckled on his club and his other hand fisted. He could take whatever insults Domitius wanted to hurl at him, but he wouldn't allow him to hurt Meg.

"Yes, Domitius, not another word. Not if you want to keep your job." Head Librarian Marco's face hardened in a way that Basil had never seen before. Marco gestured at the chaos of scurrying giant rodents and fighting librarians. "Besides, I don't think fighting amongst ourselves is the best use of our time, hmm?"

Domitius shifted, his gaze swinging away from both Basil and Marco. "No, sir."

"Good. Now, go defend the Library." Head Librarian Marco gave each of them a stern look before he clutched his club tighter, tossed his beard over his shoulder once more, then let out another war cry as he rushed off into battle again.

Shoulders hunched, Domitius raced off in a different direction.

Next to Basil, Meg hoisted her shepherd's staff. She gave him a sharp nod.

With a deep breath, Basil waded into the battle. While he, Meg, Domitius, and Head Librarian Marco had been talking, leathery bat-like creatures had joined the rodents, and these new creatures dove at the embattled librarians and bookwyrms, tugging at people's hair and slashing with sharp claws.

Grimly, Basil smashed the bats from the air, pinning them until the Library could swallow the monsters. Beside him, Meg hooked rodents with the end of her shepherd's staff and held them in place for the Library to kill and swallow.

Three bookwyrms darted around them, giving warning when a bat or rodent tried to sneak up behind them, and snapping at anything that got too close to Basil and Meg. As he and Meg fought the monsters, they worked their way into one of the side passages of shelves off the main atrium, clearing the Library of monsters one row of shelves at a time.

After what felt like an age, Basil straightened after the Library ate yet another bat creature. He swiped sweaty hair from his forehead and glanced up to the glass dome and the stars barely visible between the leaves of the indoor tree. He slumped against the shelves behind him. It wasn't even midnight yet.

Meg sighed and sagged against the bookshelves next to him. "This is quite the dust-up, isn't it?"

Basil barked a short laugh, leaning his head against the solid shelves. A twig detached from the wood and patted his shoulder, as if the Library were thanking him for his efforts to protect it. "Yes. Not every Midsummer Night is like this. Most aren't this messy."

"Good to know." Meg grimaced and swiped her hands, one at a time, on her grimy dress.

A boom shook the entire Library. Violently. An inhuman shriek of groaning wood pierced the air, ringing loud and long. The Library itself crying out in audible pain.

Basil reached for Meg as they both staggered, wincing under the weight of the Library's scream.

Meg gripped the lapels of his coat. "Skulking skunks, what was that?"

"Something terrible." Basil wrapped an arm around her waist as they stumbled around the shelves.

As the atrium came into view, Basil skidded to a halt, his grip tightening on Meg.

At the base of the great Library tree, a black vaporous hole twisted and shimmered.

Meg leaned into Basil, as if scared for the first time since this battle started. "That black thing isn't good, is it?"

"No." The end of Basil's club wavered as his hand shook. "That's not just a thin spot. That's a rift. Something has torn the barrier between our realm and the Realm of Monsters."

"So anything can start wandering through?" Meg brandished her staff, as if prepared to take on the entire Realm of Monsters by herself. "How do we close it?"

Basil opened his mouth to answer, but his words caught in his throat as something moved in the rift.

From its depths, a monster stalked into the Library. It appeared like a giant rooster with yellow, taloned feet, green-feathered body, and a yellow beak below a red, wobbling crest on top of its head. Instead of a plumed tail like a rooster, a barbed, dragon's tail whipped behind it. A pair of leathery wings rose from its back, and it flapped its wings as it crowed like a rooster, just louder and harsher than any normal chicken.

Heart hammering, Basil swung Meg off her feet and around the end of the bookshelves, hiding both of them from view.

"What…" Meg trailed off as she met Basil's gaze.

He wasn't sure what she could read on his face. He was shaking, and he held her tight as if that could keep her safe against this monster. "That's a cockatrice. It will mesmerize you with its gaze, then kill you."

Meg shuddered in Basil's arms. "Sounds awful."

"It is." Basil swallowed, pressing his face against her hair.

"My parents were killed by a cockatrice during the last bad Midsummer Night."

One of Meg's arms slipped around his neck, and she hugged him. "I'm sorry."

He heard both the sympathy and understanding in her tone. Holding her, drawing in comfort, he buried his face against her golden hair. For a moment, the groaning Library, battling librarians, snarling bookwyrms, and crowing cockatrice didn't exist.

He loved her.

And now he needed to make sure he didn't lose her tonight the way he'd lost his parents.

## CHAPTER 13

*M*eg felt the tremors in Basil. This monster had shaken him in a way that the other creatures hadn't. Understandable, given that a cockatrice had killed his parents.

Shouting filled the Library's atrium. Meg twisted in Basil's arms to peek around the end of the shelves. The double doors to the hall stood open, and Queen Hippolyta led a charge of her swordmaidens to attack the cockatrice, along with several more large monsters that had crawled through the rift. The cockatrice flapped its wings again, raking Queen Hippolyta's shield with its spurs, long talons on the back of its feet.

The action was just like the old, bad-tempered rooster Meg's family used to have—before they'd killed him and turned him into a stew.

Just a large, cantankerous rooster. That was all this monster was, at its heart. Sure, it could mesmerize with its gaze. But surely the same trick that worked on her old rooster would work on this monster.

"I have an idea." Meg looped the top of her shepherd's

crook over her shoulder, then reached inside Basil's librarian coat, digging deep into one of the lower pockets.

Basil stiffened. His breathing pressed his chest and stomach against her arm. "What are you doing?"

"I need a rope." Meg dug deeper. Her arm went into the pocket all the way to her elbow, even though the pocket looked to be only a few inches big on the outside. She angled her body to reach farther in, her shoulder against Basil's body. "Rope. Come on, Coat. I need a rope. A nice, long, sturdy rope."

Basil held still. "Why do you need a rope?"

Meg's fingers brushed the familiar, rough texture of a sisal rope. "Got it." She withdrew her arm. She gripped a large coil of an inch-thick rope. "This will do nicely."

"Do I even want to know?" Basil tugged on his lapels, straightening his coat.

"Probably not." Meg hung the rope over her shoulder with her shepherd's crook, then gripped Basil's hand once again. Strange how easy that gesture had become over the last few hours. They had been too busy not dying to worry about awkwardness.

She tugged Basil around the end of the bookshelves and ran toward the battle in the atrium. The five swordmaidens raced around the cockatrice, poking at it with their swords and spears to keep it from focusing on any one person long enough to mesmerize them.

As Queen Hippolyta stepped back to allow one of her swordmaidens to take her place, Meg skidded to a halt at her side, stuffing down any churning nerves at talking with the intimidating queen. "Your Majesty, I have an idea for how to take down the cockatrice."

Queen Hippolyta half-turned from the battle, giving Meg a better view of the spatters of blood coating the queen's leather armor. The queen's hard gaze stabbed into Meg. "Speak."

Meg took the rope from her shoulders. "We need to make a snare and loop the rope over that big branch over there." She pointed up at one of the large, lower branches of the great tree. "We need to snag both of the cockatrice's legs and hoist it off its feet. That will incapacitate it long enough for you to kill it."

Queen Hippolyta gave a sharp nod. She called for two of her swordmaidens and quickly explained what was needed.

Meg tied the knot for the loop, then handed the rope off to one of the swordmaidens. The agile warrior woman quickly had the rope tossed over the branch while the other two swordmaidens kept the cockatrice occupied.

While the warriors positioned the loop on the moss floor, Meg joined Basil, Head Librarian Marco, and every librarian that could be spared to grip the other end of the rope, braced for the signal.

Meg could only watch the battle out of the corner of her eye, not daring to look at the squawking, crowing cockatrice directly.

Queen Hippolyta dashed toward the cockatrice, prodding it with her spear before dashing away in the direction of the snare. The other swordmaidens took turns doing the same as the cockatrice flapped and lumbered after them, pecking with its beak and swiping with its talons.

One of the cockatrice's three-toed feet stepped into the snare. The rope in Meg's hands tensed as some of the librarians behind her began tugging.

"Not yet." Meg held the rope in place, Basil's strength at her back lending her courage.

Queen Hippolyta swiped at the cockatrice, then danced back a step. She held still, brandishing her sword and glaring directly at the cockatrice.

The cockatrice took one more step, firmly placing both feet within the noose of the snare. With Queen Hippolyta standing still, the cockatrice halted, swinging its head to gaze back at the queen to mesmerize her.

Queen Hippolyta's risk in using herself as bait gave them the chance they needed.

"Now!" Meg yanked on the rope as hard as she could. Behind her, the librarians hauled on the rope.

The loop tightened around the cockatrice's ankles. Then the creature was hoisted off its feet to dangle upside down. The cockatrice's beak fell open, and it let out a continuous squawking even as it squeezed its eyes shut. Its wings flopped open and hung there, splayed and awkward. Just like the rooster used to do back home when snagged by its feet and carried, utterly helpless.

Shaking herself free of the last effects of the cockatrice's mesmerizing gaze, Queen Hippolyta raised her sword, braced herself, and swung.

Meg squeezed her eyes shut and turned away. Blood and gore didn't bother her, exactly. But this was a whole lot bigger and bloodier than simply dispatching a chicken for the pot back on the farm.

The squawking cut off, and Meg let the rope drop from her hands. The sound of a large body thunking on the floor filled the room.

With a deep breath, Meg forced herself to open her eyes and face the battlefield. While they had been dealing with the cockatrice, another of those goat-lion-snake creatures—chimera she had thought she'd heard it called—crawled through the rift, followed by another wave of large rodents.

"We need to close that rift." Meg hefted her shepherd's staff again. As long as that rift remained open, they were never going to win. The monsters would just keep coming, while those defending the Library would just get weaker and more exhausted. "Unless…will it close on its own as soon as the sun rises?"

"That is one possibility, but I don't think we have the time to wait for that." Basil wrapped an arm around Meg's waist and tugged her to a sheltered spot formed by a curving set of bookshelves. "There was something I wanted to try." He cupped her chin, then leaned closer, the look in his eyes soft. "If you don't mind."

What was…? Meg's heart hammered, her breath catching in her chest. Was he…?

Basil kissed her. Full on the mouth and everything.

For a moment, Meg was too surprised, too overwhelmed by the new sensation, to do more than stand there. Then, she leaned into Basil, her legs growing weak as a delicious warmth spread through her.

When Basil drew back, all she could do was grip his shirt, her thoughts muddled. Perhaps that was why she blurted the first thing that came to her. "Kissing in the middle of a battle is a little cliché, isn't it?"

Basil's mouth quirked. "Maybe. But I thought if evil and anger can tear a rift, then surely love can repair it. And the traditions always say that a first kiss is an especially powerful binding, after all."

Meg glanced over her shoulder. Was the rift a little smaller than it had been? Or was that just wishful thinking? She turned back to Basil, tugging him down to her again. "In that case, we'd better try again. I don't think one kiss was enough."

She kissed him this time. Longer. Deeper.

This would explain why people liked kissing so much. It was rather pleasant. Especially with someone who made her feel the way Basil did.

Something clunked into the top of her head. She pushed back from Basil and glanced up.

Puck perched on the bookshelf behind Basil. The sprite plucked another book and hurled it, hitting the back of Basil's head. "Librarian Basil! This is no time for kissing!"

Basil rubbed the back of his head. "Puck? What are you doing here?"

The others had gone back to fighting, too busy dispatching monsters to pay any attention to her and Basil or to the barely-clothed sprite chucking books from the shelves. The rift was still there, a vaporous and twisting thing, though no more large monsters had come through. Perhaps her and Basil's kissing hadn't sealed the rift, but it might have held back the tide of monsters, at least for a time.

That was what she would tell herself. It was as good an excuse as any for wasting time kissing while everyone else was fighting desperately for their lives.

Puck dropped down from the shelves to land at their feet. Five gashes cut across his chest, his darker green blood standing out against the brighter emerald of his skin. Patches of his leaf loincloth were smudged with dirt and soaked with the evergreen-colored blood.

"Are you all right?" Meg stepped closer to the sprite. He was an annoying imp, but he had clearly been hurt. Apparently the Library recognized the same thing, for it didn't so much as smack Puck for throwing books from the shelves or dirtying the floor with his blood.

"Nevermind me." The sprite clasped his hands, falling to his knees before Basil. "Please, Librarian Basil! The Court of Revels needs your help. I have made a grave mistake!"

Basil sighed, glancing over his shoulder at the battle as if he, too, felt guilty that they had abandoned the others for so long. "Can this wait?"

"No! It's about the battle!" Puck reached forward and grasped the end of Basil's coat. "A rift has opened all the way here from the Court of Revels, and it is all my fault!"

## CHAPTER 14

*B*asil sucked in a breath, mind whirling. "What happened?"

He couldn't imagine a rift that large. What could Puck possibly have done to rip such a tear in the barrier?

Puck was shaking, his yellow eyes wide. "It's terrible! So terrible! Monsters are flooding into both our Courts. I barely made it here alive."

"That does sound dreadful." Meg knelt on the moss floor next to Puck, her tone soothing. "Why don't you explain to us exactly what happened? From the beginning?"

She had far more self-control and sense than Basil did at the moment. Right now, he wanted to shake the explanation out of Puck.

Puck swung his gaze to her, as if latching onto the calm in Meg's voice. He let go of Basil's coat and instead reached for Meg's sleeve.

To her credit, she didn't flinch away, even though Puck's fingers were covered with dirt and flakes of dried, green blood.

Puck drew in a deep breath and let it out with a shudder.

"My King Oberon wanted to get revenge on Queen Titania. She was doting on a child she adopted, and King Oberon was jealous of the time she was spending on the boy instead of with him. So, he planned, on Midsummer Night, to spell her to fall in love with someone unsuitable and ridiculous."

Meg's eyebrows shot up. "Let me get this straight. King Oberon purposefully used magic to make his wife cheat on him, as revenge on her. Does anyone else see how this doesn't make any sense?"

"That's King Oberon and Queen Titania for you." Basil shrugged and crossed his arms, trying to hold back the growing pressure inside his chest. There was a rift spilling monsters into his Court, and he was stuck here listening to Puck's rambling explanation.

"Who can understand the mind of my great King Oberon?" Puck smirked, but then the expression faltered. "Anyway, King Oberon threw away the page with the anti-dote flower, saying that we wouldn't need it. Tonight, he carried out his plan. Queen Titania was spelled to fall in love with a donkey-headed man, and he with her."

Basil's stomach dropped. "No, don't tell me. The donkey-headed man is Nick Bottom. But he's from the Court of Knowledge, not the Court of Revels. King Oberon promised he wouldn't use the love flower on anyone outside of his own Court."

"Yes, but we didn't know!" Puck threw his hands in the air. "We just saw an acting troupe practicing in the Tangle-wood, and of course we assumed they belonged to the Court of Revels. And Nick Bottom was just so perfectly ridiculous, we couldn't help it."

Basil resisted the urge to roll his eyes. Buddy was right. King Oberon and Queen Titania were definitely the Deplorable Duo. Bad enough that they involved their own Court in such shenanigans, but to pull in someone from another Court went against all the rules that governed the Fae Realm.

But was that enough to tear such a rift in the barrier to the Realm of Monsters? King Oberon had pulled stunts like this before, and it hadn't caused this much chaos. Though, he'd never done it on such a perilous Midsummer Night before.

No matter. They'd have to fix it. Basil drew himself straighter. "Then we'll look up the antidote flower again, find the flower, and undo what King Oberon has done to Queen Titania and Nick Bottom. That should heal the rift, I hope."

Even before Basil finished speaking, Puck was shaking his head. "No, no. That won't do. Or, at least, that's not all of it. Nick Bottom's situation didn't create the rift. It might have contributed to thinning a spot, but it didn't make the tear. After all, my great King Oberon promised that he would not use the knowledge gained on someone *in* another Court, not someone *from* another Court. At the time, Bottom and the other players were practicing over the border in the Court of Revels, even though they didn't know they had crossed into that side of the Tanglewood."

Basil clenched his fists. King Oberon and his semantics. "Then what happened to cause the rift?"

"Well, I…" Puck wouldn't look at either of them as he shifted, scuffing his bare foot on the moss floor. "King Oberon and I went to observe the Revel—it is such fun, you see. And we saw Hermia, Lysander, Helena, and Demetrius. They were arguing and chasing each other, and poor Helena seemed so miserable."

"Surely you didn't." Basil braced himself on the shelves.

Puck went on as if he hadn't heard him. "King Oberon didn't think it would matter if we helped the Revel along a little, and we had more of the love flower. And the four were on the Court of Revels side of the Tanglewood, so it technically didn't violate his promise."

"You messed with the magic of the Revel." Basil couldn't comprehend how even Puck and King Oberon could be so foolish.

Still kneeling on the floor, Meg glanced between Puck and Basil. "Why would that cause all this?" She gestured in the direction of the continuing battle. Queen Hippolyta yelled a war cry as she stabbed down at a giant, three-headed snake.

Basil rubbed a hand over his face. "It was bad enough that King Oberon worked enchantments on five members of another Court, nevermind his arguments to his innocence. But worse, he interfered with the Midsummer Revel, a magical tradition that is foundational to his Court."

He just shook his head. Even with good intentions, which were always questionable when it came to King Oberon, the king should have known better. The Revel was held in the Tanglewood—mythical enchanted forest that it was—because the magic of the forest had a way of sorting things into the way they were meant to be. If left alone, Demetrius probably would have been brought to see reason or Helena would have figured out how to let him go or however they were meant to end up.

Now King Oberon and Puck had broken that.

"But then they got all mixed up, and the more times we tried to fix it, the worse everything got, and the rift opened, and everything went horribly wrong!" Puck wailed the last word, throwing up his hands and plopping onto the floor.

"You interfered with the Revel *multiple times*!" Basil couldn't keep his voice from rising. No wonder a rift had been torn through the barrier.

Meg reached up and tugged on his coat. "Basil. Calm down. We are supposed to be the rational ones here."

Basil inhaled and exhaled slowly, trying to ease the pounding at his temples and the tension squeezing his chest. "Right. Of course."

"Correct me if I'm wrong, but I think our plan is still the same." Meg pushed to her feet and picked up her staff. "We find the flower we need to undo the other flower, then we cure everybody who has been love-spelled out of their wits, and that should seal the rift, right?"

"Yes." Basil lifted his own club. He hoped that was all it would take. King Oberon had torn into the very power of how the Court of Revels functioned. If he and Meg had not only to fix the love spells but also fix Oberon and Titania's marriage…

Then they were all doomed. Very, very, *very* doomed.

Basil couldn't dwell on that now. "Let's find that book."

With Meg and Puck following him, Basil led the way deeper into the Library. They had to pause several times to fight off more of those rodents and bat-creatures. But, finally, they reached the shelf that held the books on magical plants.

Basil rested his hand on the wood of the Library's shelf. He could feel the whole Library trembling, as if the building were in pain from the rift torn in its heart. "I know this is a lot to ask, Great Library. But we need the book with the magical love flower and its antidote in order to fix all of this. Please."

The Library's shudder shook the moss beneath their feet. A groan filled the air as a branch separated from one of the higher shelves and, slowly, achingly, it plucked a book from the shelf and held it out to Basil.

Basil ran his hand over the Library's branch. "Thank you."

"Yes, thank you." Meg joined Basil and gently touched the branch, as if trying to soothe the Library's agony.

Basil flipped through the book as quickly as possible until

he found the page with the love flower. One more page, and he was looking at the white antidote flower. "Here it is. Now we just have to find it."

He scanned the page, searching for the section on where the flower grew and best harvesting methods to preserve its magic.

Meg leaned over his arm, her head partially blocking his view. "I've seen that flower before. There's some in the protected glade connected to your Anywhere Door."

"Really? You sure?" Basil leaned away from her, trying to peer around her to see the illustration.

Meg straightened and gave him a *look*. "Of course I'm sure. I'm a farmgirl. I notice things like plants. You might know a lot of things, Basil, but observing the world around you isn't your strong point."

It wasn't? Basil glanced from her to the book, then nodded. If Meg said the flower was in the clearing, then it was there. He closed the book and handed it back to the Library's branch.

Trembling, the Library returned the book, the branch falling limp rather than retracting back into the shelf.

They didn't have any time to waste. Basil spun on his heel. Puck stood only a few feet behind him. For once, the sprite had kept his hands to himself and he hadn't started chucking books from the shelves or tearing up the moss or anything else destructive.

"Puck." Basil tried to put as much command into his tone as possible. "I need you to run ahead to the Tanglewood and locate Hermia, Lysander, Helena, and Demetrius. Try to round them up into one place. That will make it easier for us to undo the love flower when Meg and I get there with the antidote."

"Yes, sir!" Puck flourished something that might have

been an attempt at a salute. Puck spun and hustled off, bounding off the shelves, until he disappeared out of sight.

"Do you think he can be trusted to actually track down those four?" Meg waved in the direction that Puck had gone.

"Probably not." Basil shrugged, steadying himself as the Library gave another pained tremor. "But it is better than having him underfoot while we retrieve the antidote flower."

"Good point." Meg grimaced. Then she swatted her staff at a scuttling crab monster that had found its way into their corner. "Let's go."

Basil took a step, then hesitated. His mind whirled. "I probably should explain to King Theseus and Queen Hippolyta what is going on. They need to know."

"Of course." Meg faced him, then smoothed one of his lapels. "I can find my way through the Anywhere Door to the glade. I'll get the flower while you report to your king and queen."

Basil didn't want to agree. He didn't like the thought of Meg going off by herself on this night of all nights, especially not with a rift open to the Realm of Monsters spewing out who knew what foul creatures into all of the Court of Knowledge.

But he had to trust her. She had faced down the cockatrice and come up with the plan to defeat it. She was probably better equipped for fighting monsters than he was.

"All right. I'll meet you at the House. Just…" Basil reached out and traced her cheek with the back of his hand. "Stay safe."

Meg huffed and shook her head. "That's the plan."

The plan. Somehow, this night didn't seem one for depending on plans going right.

## CHAPTER 15

*M*eg sprinted through the Library's atrium. Past the knots of embattled librarians and valiant warrior women fighting against monster after monster. Out of the corner of her eye, she could see Basil skidding to a halt next to Queen Hippolyta, gesturing and speaking loudly enough that Meg could hear his voice, even if she couldn't make out his words.

She reached the large double doors and flung one open. On the other side, King Theseus and more of the sword-maidens held back an onslaught of monsters.

Even as Meg stepped inside, the floor beneath her seemed to tilt. A ripping sound filled the air, then one of the black, misty holes twisted into existence in the middle of the hall.

King Theseus gave a shout, and the fighting men and women raced toward him, even as their eyes widened and fear crossed their faces.

The rift was growing. It wasn't a continuous tear, but it was like a slash in a piece of fabric where some of the threads still remained, holding the material together, while a line of holes formed along the cut. But, eventually, those last threads would break, and the smaller holes would become one large hole.

She couldn't allow that to happen. Not to her new home. Not when she finally had the chance to give her siblings a better life.

Not when she had Basil.

A roar filled the air as a truly massive creature slithered from the rift.

She couldn't turn from her path now. She dodged past the knot of warriors, jumped over a rodent, ducked a swooping taloned bat, and weaved around the whipping tail of some other monster.

Her fingers grasped the handle of the Door that connected to the House since the Anywhere Door in the Library didn't connect directly to the glade. She willed it to bring her home, even as she yanked it open. Without even looking first, she threw herself inside.

She stumbled into the House, its moss floor and cozy walls wrapping around her. For a moment, all she wanted to do was slump to the floor and soak up the illusion of safety this cottage provided.

But, echoing from outside the House, the sound of Buddy's snort and the smashing sound of his hooves against something solid proved the House wasn't as safe as it seemed.

Meg spun and slammed the Anywhere Door shut behind her with more force than she'd intended.

The House gave a huffy shake, and dirt crumbled onto Meg's head.

"Sorry, sorry. I didn't mean it." Meg gripped the handle to the Anywhere Door. "Please. I need you to behave tonight, all right? I'm trying to save everyone."

When she jerked the Door open, it showed the quiet glade. After the chaos of the last few hours of battle, the glade's peaceful, moss-covered ground and chuckling stream seemed too perfect, too pristine, too unreal.

Meg stumbled into the glade, casting about for the flowers.

There. Growing in tufts at the base of one of the willow trees.

She grabbed a handful, careful to leave a few flowers still growing and not tear the plant up by the roots. She didn't want to accidentally destroy their means to stop that love flower again in the future. For some reason, she didn't think even this would teach Puck, King Oberon, and Queen Titania their lesson.

She spun on her heel and raced back the way she'd come, this time taking the time to shut the Anywhere Door properly. Basil would need it shut to come through in a few minutes, once he finished explaining everything at the Library.

Roars and clattering hooves rang from outside the House. Buddy's trumpeting war cry joined the clamor.

Picking up her staff once again, she hurried for the front door. She and Basil would need Buddy to take them to the Tanglewood. There wasn't an Anywhere Door that would go straight there.

Meg cracked the door open, peeking outside. All she could see was Buddy's round, brown pony butt.

At least that was better than a monster right outside the door.

"Buddy." She pulled the door the rest of the way open and patted Buddy's flank to let him know she was there.

Buddy's head swung around to glance over his back at her. "Meg? What are you doing here?"

"Long story." Meg raised her staff and swatted aside yet another of those bat monsters. "Short version, King Oberon opened a rift to the Realm of Monsters, and Basil and I need to fix it by saving the Foolish Four from a love spell. And possibly Nick Bottom as well. Puck was a little unclear on exactly what had happened to him."

"Got it." Buddy whirled, then kicked with both of his rear legs, sending a larger lion creature tumbling and whimpering. "That would explain this mess, if the Foolish Four got mixed up with the Deplorable Duo. That's a recipe for disaster."

"To put it mildly." Meg kicked away from the scurrying rodents. "This is only going to get worse until we close that rift."

Buddy didn't bother to respond. He was too busy lashing out with his hooves, keeping another wave of creeping, crawling monsters at bay.

The door opened behind Meg, and Basil stepped out, gripping his club. "Did you get the flowers?"

"Yes." Meg held up her handful of white flowers. "I take it King Theseus and Queen Hippolyta know what's going on?"

Basil nodded. "They're trying to figure out a way to protect the most people. Queen Hippolyta's reinforcements are pouring through the Anywhere Door from her Court as we speak. They're planning to deploy into the village to protect as many people as possible."

"Good." Meg rested her hand on the doorpost. "I'm sorry, House. But we're going to have to leave you undefended while we fix this."

It was a small thing, after Queen Hippolyta was leaving her entire island under-defended to protect the Court of Knowledge. But Meg had to swallow back a lump in her throat at the thought that something might happen to the House.

The House gave a shudder under her hand, but she didn't think it was a plea for them to stay. More fear, but also understanding. As Basil had explained, the House wasn't exactly sentient. It wasn't a person, though it had a form of a personality. All it wished was to protect and serve those who lived inside its walls.

With another groan of stone and wood, the walls closed around the door and the windows. In moments, the House was nothing but four solid stone walls, as impenetrable as it could be.

"I guess that's our cue." Buddy swiveled to them. "Hurry. Get on before another wave of monsters attacks."

Meg scrambled onto Buddy's back, still gripping the flowers tightly in one hand. When Basil climbed onto Buddy behind her, he wrapped one arm around her waist. She leaned against him, the muscles of his chest behind her and the warmth of his arm far more natural than they had felt when he had been a stranger, carrying her off into this unknown realm.

The two of them were a heavy load for Buddy. Probably heavier than he should carry since he was a pony, not a full-sized horse.

But he gamely broke into a gallop, tearing down the street. As a pony, Buddy didn't have the long-legged, ground-eating stride of a horse. Instead, he charged in a full-tilt, leg-pumping, short gait that felt like holding onto a flooding, whitewater river.

Meg gripped Buddy's sides with her legs, holding tight. Basil's weight nearly dragged her off the back of the pony, if not for her grip. Sitting farther back as he was, he was jostled more than she was. Still, he held on as best he could, lashing out at any monsters that got too close to Buddy.

Meg would have also lashed out, but she was too busy clutching Buddy's mane and the precious flowers. If she lost those flowers, this would all be for nothing.

Even as they raced through the village, a black rift shivered across the streets and houses to their right.

"The rift is getting worse," Basil shouted into her ear.

"Yeah, I can see that." Meg leaned lower over Buddy's neck. His thick mane lashed at her face with each stride.

Buddy's eyes remained focused forward, his nostrils flared as wide as they would go as he heaved great gulps of air. His neck and chest were rapidly darkening with sweat.

Ahead, the Tanglewood stretched black and looming in the darkness of night. The forest itself almost appeared to be a rift, growing larger and larger, until it looked like it would swallow them whole.

Buddy plunged into the trees without slowing his pace. He stumbled over the uneven ground, but he kept charging forward.

Branches slashed at Meg's face, stinging her eyes. She hunched over the white flowers to protect them.

How big was this forest? Even assuming that Puck had managed to round up Hermia, Helena, Lysander, and Demetrius in that short amount of time, how were they supposed to find them in here?

Meg glanced over her shoulder. "Which way should we go?"

Basil's grip tightened around her waist. When he answered her, he shouted loudly enough for Buddy to hear as well, "Just keep going straight on. We need to trust in the magic of the Tanglewood to bring us exactly where we need to be."

"But what if the magic of the Tanglewood has been damaged by what Puck and King Oberon did?" Meg resisted the urge to squeeze the flowers tighter. She didn't want to crush the stems too badly, in case they were important.

"They damaged the magical tradition of the Midsummer Revel." Even at a shout, Basil's tone took on that lecturing tone that Meg found both annoying and endearing, in an odd way. Basil wouldn't be Basil if he didn't lecture occasionally.

"Yes, the magic of the Revel is connected to the Tanglewood, but the Tanglewood is far older, far more powerful than a mere tradition created by the Court of Revels, though they made sure that their tradition aligned with the Tanglewood's power. And, for that reason, the Tanglewood will want to assert its power both within its borders and over the Revel once again."

"If I'm understanding all that right, it's in the forest's best interest to take us right to them." Meg faced forward again, though she rested the hand gripping the flowers against Basil's arm around her waist.

"I wish…the forest…would hurry." Buddy gasped between deep breaths. "Duck!"

Meg pressed herself to Buddy's neck, Basil's weight settling against her back, as they both ducked. A low-hanging branch flashed over their heads.

Buddy burst through what seemed like a wall of greenery. Then he braced his legs, going from a gallop to a halt.

Meg nearly flew over his neck. Only the strength of her legs and her braced arm on Buddy's neck saved both her and Basil from taking a tumble.

Puck stood in the middle of a clearing, hands on his hips.

Basil slid to the ground. "Have you found them?"

"Yes, but they keep running off every time I try to round them up." Puck flapped his hands, the picture of indignant exasperation.

Meg eased to the ground as well. Her skirt and leggings were damp and rimed with white salt from Buddy's sweat. Foam covered his neck and chest, and his head hung low as he gulped great breaths.

"You are the most valiant steed in all of the Fae Realm." Meg patted Buddy's shoulder. The talking pony had given his all to gallop her and Basil that far, that fast. Meg hoped he hadn't permanently injured himself at all.

Buddy didn't respond, still gasping deep breaths, his sides heaving.

Basil ran his hand through his hair, grimacing. "We'll have to split up. It will be faster. Meg, could you please give one of the flowers to Puck?"

Fighting her own urge to grimace, Meg handed a flower to the sprite. She still had four in her hand, which should be more than enough for everyone, even if Puck messed up his task.

Smirking, Puck took the flower and stuffed it into the waistband of his loincloth until only its white flower head remained visible, bobbing with each of his movements. "Ta-ta for now! I shall track down the wayward lovers and get this straightened out in no time at all!"

Puck bounded up a tree, then vanished among the foliage.

"Why do I get the feeling he's only going to make things worse?" Meg sighed, flexing her grip on the remaining flowers. Her hand was cramping from all the tension, even if gripping flowers wasn't that physically demanding. "But, like before, it at least keeps him busy."

"Exactly." Basil glanced at Buddy, then held out his hand to Meg. "Let's see if we can find any of them. Buddy, stay here and rest."

As Buddy nodded, Meg took Basil's hand. Together, the two of them set out into the Tanglewood in the opposite direction that Puck had gone.

The tramping of their boots on the loam provided a pleasant rhythm. The nighttime forest smelled of sweet greenery and damp earth in a heady scent. Mists swirled beneath the canopy, cold and clammy against Meg's arms. Strange lights blinked on and off in the distance. Occasionally, disembodied giggles came from deeper into the forest. Sometimes even a shriek or muffled voices.

Meg hoped those were the other fae participating in the

Revel or part of the enchantment of the forest, and not some monster that had crawled from the rift.

Basil's fingers tightened around hers. "I snatched you so that I wouldn't end up in the Tanglewood on Midsummer Night. At least I don't have to participate in the Revel."

Despite their dire situation, she found herself grinning. "Nope. You're already stuck with me. Instead, you're here to stop a rift from tearing apart your Court and destroying the Fae Realm. So much better."

Basil laughed under his breath, a smile breaking the hard lines that had set into his face over the past few hours. "I'm glad I have you with me. This would have been terrible, trying to stop Puck's tomfoolery on my own."

"You would still be trying to figure out where the white flowers grow." Meg squeezed his fingers in return to make sure he knew her words were mere gentle teasing.

"And the cockatrice might have hurt someone before it had been dispatched." Basil's mouth quirked even more than it had before.

A scream pierced the forest, ringing far louder than the distant noises of before.

"That's Lysander." Basil broke into a run, tugging Meg along with him.

"How do you know what Lysander screams like?" Meg kept pace with him, doing her best not to trip over the large roots protruding through the moss- and loam-covered forest floor.

"Last Midsummer Night. Less chaotic than this one, but enough monsters invaded the Library to make it interesting." Basil managed to shrug while running. "And Lysander is a screamer, though Helena still has him beat when it comes to ear-piercing pitch."

They turned a corner around a massive tree, then skidded to a halt. Before them, Lysander, his dark hair and clothes covered with dried mud, gripped a stick as he faced a gigantic snake-creature, its mouth gaping open to reveal fangs dripping with a purple liquid that had to be venom. Its slitted eyes narrowed as it focused on Lysander.

Lysander wasn't moving. He was far too still, the stick not wavering.

Hermia stood behind him, gripping Lysander's shoulders and sobbing into his back, her body shaking.

"Seething snakes, what *is* that thing?" Meg gaped at the creature before them. Of all the monsters they had faced that night, this one—with its scales so darkly purple they were nearly black and its dripping fangs—seemed the most sinister.

"A basilisk." Basil's fingers clutched Meg's hand so tightly that it hurt.

"Great. Another new monster." Meg blew out a long breath. She probably shouldn't make light of the situation, but it was either that or break down shaking like Hermia. "Does that Library of yours have a book of monsters or something to reference? Because I think I might want to learn to read just so I can study up for next Midsummer's Night. Or any other time thin spots appear and unleash monsters on the Courts."

Basil's tense expression didn't change. "A basilisk isn't just any new monster. It freezes anyone who looks into its eyes and, unlike a cockatrice, there is no way to fight the effects and it doesn't end the moment the beast looks away. The basilisk's fangs also have deadly poison that kills slowly and painfully."

"Got it." Meg placed her back to the tree, tucking herself farther out of sight. "How do we kill it?"

"If Lysander wasn't about to be eaten, I'd say the best way would be to wait for Queen Hippolyta's swordmaidens. They are the ones trained to fight monsters like this." Basil swiped his free hand on his trousers, his skin graying beneath his tan.

In other words, Basil wasn't sure what to do. Meg tucked the flowers into a crook of the tree, then faced him. "It's basically a very big, very deadly snake, right? Back home, we would pin rattlesnakes to the ground with a forked stick, then someone else could safely lop its head off."

"You make that sound so doable." Basil shook his head, glanced around the tree, and winced. "We don't have much time. How do we pull this off?"

"I'll need an ax. Can your coat conjure one of those up?" Meg searched the trees around them.

There. A few feet away, a low-hanging limb branched into a sturdy fork the right size for pinning the basilisk.

Basil dug into one of the pockets of his coat and pulled out a large, single-headed ax like she would use for chopping wood.

Meg reached for it. "Perfect. Can you give me a boost so I can chop down that branch?"

Basil held the ax out of her reach. "This is an enchanted forest. It won't appreciate you taking an ax to it. And, at this point, we don't want to annoy the Tanglewood. We have enough problems."

"Then how am I supposed to get that forked branch? Ask the forest nicely?" Meg tamped down the rising anger. They didn't have time to argue.

"Actually, yes." Basil glanced around the tree again, then groaned. "We are out of time. I need to help Hermia distract the basilisk. Get that branch and do what you have to do." He held out the ax.

"No, you keep it. Once I get the basilisk pinned, I'll need you to chop off its head." Meg hesitated. Should they hug? Kiss? Do something to mark this moment since they were both probably going to die?

From somewhere behind the tree came a short scream.

Basil's grip tightened on his ax, then he turned and raced around the tree.

Meg placed her hand on the tree. "Please, Tree. I need that forked branch. It is life or death. If we're going to stop this monster, save Lysander and Hermia, and close the rift, then I need this branch."

She willed the tree to cooperate, even knowing that when it came to willpower, this ancient enchanted forest had far more than she did. Meg was a mere speck against its power.

But she needed this branch. There was no other option. The Tanglewood had to bend. Had to listen to her.

Something thumped to the ground.

When Meg peeled her eyes open, the forked branch lay on the moss. All ends looked as if they had been neatly sliced from the tree, even cleaner than she would have been able to do with an ax. The Tanglewood had nicely shaped it to the perfect size for what Meg needed.

"Thank you." Meg patted the tree's trunk. Even as she stood there, the nub where the forked branch had been started regrowing.

No time to stand there watching a branch grow. Meg scooped up her weapon, gritting her teeth at its weight. This was larger than the small sticks she had used on the snakes back home.

Though, this poisonous serpent was much bigger as well.

Instead of following Basil around the tree, Meg circled through the forest. She needed to come at the basilisk from behind.

A hissing sound filled the air, followed by unintelligible shouting from both Basil and Hermia.

Meg's heart hammered, but she drew in deep breaths to steady herself. Basil would be fine. He had to be fine.

She eased through the undergrowth to peek into the clearing for the first time.

The basilisk's tail flicked back and forth only a few feet away from her. The coils of its body filled the space beneath the large trees.

Basil jumped out of the way as the basilisk lunged. He swiped with the ax, hitting its jaw. The basilisk hissed, and its mouth gaped wider.

Lysander remained exactly where he was, frozen in place, but Hermia crouched off to the side, waiting to dodge away from the basilisk again.

Meg tiptoed forward, holding her breath as her heart thundered. Could the basilisk hear her heartbeat?

Basil glanced to her, then focused back on the monster. Both he and Hermia kept moving, dividing the beast's attention.

Meg crept closer. One step. Two steps. Three.

Something snapped beneath her foot. Loudly.

The basilisk's head started to swing in her direction.

Meg froze, gripping the branch. No, no. She needed the snake facing away from her for this to work.

Basil lunged forward and struck with the ax, burying it in the snake's neck.

The basilisk hissed and swung back to Basil in a blink.

He tried to yank out the ax, but it was buried too deep, and the basilisk too fast.

The basilisk struck. Basil cried out, falling backwards.

No, no, no. Meg couldn't even cry out. Or move.

Basil…

## CHAPTER 16

*M*eg tightened her grip on the branch and forced herself forward. This was the right moment. The basilisk was stretched out, its head low to the ground. She wouldn't have a better chance than this.

With a lunge, Meg stabbed down with the forked branch as hard as she could. Each side of the Y stabbed into the moss, pinning the basilisk's head in place. It twisted and yanked, but Meg held on. If the basilisk got free, they would all die.

The monster's huge body flailed, knocking into Meg from behind. She braced herself. "Basil! Hermia! Chop off its head! Now!"

Basil pushed to his elbow, pressing a hand to his stomach. Blood welled between his fingers, darkening his coat and staining his shirt red. He was in no shape for killing anything.

With a piercing screech, Hermia yanked the ax out of the basilisk's neck, then hacked at the monster with a feverish, wild vengeance.

The basilisk curled tighter in on itself, and Meg had to lean onto the stick to keep the monster pinned down.

Hermia swung the ax again and again, her face twisted in a look of avenging fury. She whacked and hacked and swung until the basilisk lay limp, its head completely severed from its body.

Breathing hard, Hermia halted, and her gaze swung up to meet Meg's.

Meg let go of the forked branch, and it thumped onto the basilisk's body. She hadn't had much of a chance to get to know Hermia, but perhaps they could become friends, once everything settled down.

"What happened? Where's my darling Helena?" Lysander's voice broke the stillness. Hermia dropped the ax, spun on her heel, and raced to him.

Meg tripped around the basilisk's head and fell to her knees at Basil's side. She lifted his coat. "How bad is it? Did the basilisk bite you? What can we do?"

He couldn't die. He just couldn't. This was supposed to be her new home, her new life. She had decided to embrace this crazy Fae Realm with all its quirks. She was even willing to learn to read.

Basil winced as he pushed himself higher onto his elbow. "Yes, it bit me. I need a plant. A white, star-shaped flower with a gold center. There should be some growing here in the Tanglewood. It will help slow the poison until I can get to one of the healers."

"Can't we just reach into a coat pocket and fetch one that way?" Meg pressed her hands to Basil's wounds, leaning her weight onto him to try to stop the bleeding.

He moaned, squeezing his eyes shut. "No. The coat only pulls in non-living items that have been made in some way. Like prepared food or an ax or rope. But no plants or people."

He was dying, and he still managed a full three-sentence lecture on the properties of his coat. She would find it funny, if he wasn't poisoned and bleeding out.

"Fine. I'll fetch it. Star-shaped flower. White with a gold center. I'll be back soon." Meg jumped to her feet, only to have Lysander nearly run her over, Hermia clinging to his arm.

"Lysander! Please! I don't understand! Why don't you love me anymore? I just killed a basilisk. For you!" Hermia dug in her heels, glancing over at Meg as if pleading for help.

Basil groaned, then waved toward the tree where Meg had stashed the flowers. "Better help them first. I can wait a few more minutes. The basilisk's poison is very slow-acting."

How he could sound so calm about that, Meg didn't know.

She raced for the tree, retrieved an antidote flower, then ran back. Lysander hadn't moved far, and he was blinking down at Basil as if some logical part of him, deep down, was fighting the love spell to try to override its effects on him.

Meg held up the flower. "What do I do with it?"

Basil shifted to press both hands to his stomach. "Squeeze a drop of the nectar into each of his eyes."

"Got it." Meg advanced on Lysander. "Hermia, hold him still. He's been love-spelled by Puck, and I'm going to fix it."

Hermia's eyes widened, then lit. She gripped Lysander's arm with the same fierce strength she'd shown when lopping off the basilisk's head.

Meg gripped Lysander's chin, but he wrenched his head out of her grip.

"What are you doing?" He tried to pull away from Hermia, writhing to keep his face turned away from Meg.

"This is for your own good." Hermia's jaw stuck out in a determined scowl as she dug her fingers into Lysander's hair and yanked his head back, pinning him in place.

Meg squeezed the flower's head, and a drop of clear, sparkling liquid fell from the flower into Lysander's eye. He writhed even harder, but Hermia held tight. Meg held the flower over his other eye and administered the second drop.

Lysander stilled, blinking furiously. Then, something in his face cleared, as if a curtain had fallen away to reveal morning sunlight. "Ouch! Hermia, my love. What's going on?"

Hermia released him and threw her arms around him, letting out something between a laugh and a sob. "Lysander! Dear Lysander! You're mine again!"

A little over-dramatic, but Meg couldn't fault Hermia. It must have been rather awful, to have Lysander suddenly stop loving her for no explainable reason.

Still, Basil didn't have time for this. Meg dropped back to her knees at Basil's side, then glanced over her shoulder at a now kissing couple. "Hey. Hermia. Lysander. Snap out of it. Basil needs help."

Hermia pushed back from Lysander first, glancing over at them. Her eyes widened in her flushed face. "Basil! How could I have forgotten?"

Lysander blinked, then his gaze sharpened, and he dropped to his knees on the other side of Basil. "Bas, what can we do to help?"

It was to his credit that he didn't ask for an explanation of what had happened while he was under the love spell and frozen by the basilisk. Instead, he had immediately turned to Basil, which showed even more sense.

Basil's face had paled, and beads of sweat dotted his forehead. He opened his mouth, then coughed, his face twisting in pain.

Meg rested a hand on his shoulder, not sure how much comfort her touch provided. "He told me he needs a white flower with a gold center, and that the flower will help slow the spread of the poison until we can get him to a healer. Let's spread out and hope the Tanglewood provides a flower quickly."

"Stay here with Basil. We'll find the flower." Hermia took Lysander's hand, pulling him to his feet. Together, they sprinted into the Tanglewood's depths, their clasped hands glowing with their newly formed binding, leaving Meg alone with Basil and the dead body of the giant snake monster.

Basil tried to sit up, groaned, and flopped back to the moss.

"Don't try to move." Meg eased back his coat, then tugged his hands away from the wound. Red blood still dribbled through the tear in his shirt.

She needed to bandage the wound to stop the bleeding until they could get Basil to a healer. Life on the farm had given her a basic idea of first aid and a stomach to handle gushing blood.

"Meg…" Basil reached up with shaking fingers, touching her arm. "I need to tell you…"

"Rest. You can tell me later." Meg dug into one of the pockets of Basil's coat. Instead of bandages, her fingers closed around the hilt of a knife. Not what she was hoping for, but she could work with it. She pulled it free of the pocket, then gripped the tear in Basil's shirt. "Hold still."

Basil kept talking, as if he didn't hear her. "Before we left, I asked Buddy to look after you if something happened to me tonight."

Meg sawed through his shirt, cutting a large swathe of the fabric. The puncture wound was about an inch wide, and purple streaks already spread out from the wound, discoloring Basil's skin. "Don't talk like that. You're going to be fine."

"But you need to know." Basil's gaze swung to her, more intense and alert than a moment ago. "You'll have a home, no matter what. You're my mate. The House is yours for as long as you want it. You'll still be able to bring your family here and take care of them. You'll be safe."

Meg's hand stilled, one hand gripping the knife, the other tangled in a sliced section of his shirt.

How had she managed to be snatched by the kindest, most considerate fae in this entire realm? Here he was hurt, possibly dying, and he was letting her know that she would still have everything she had wanted when she'd run away. A home. A safe place for her sisters and brother. All the food and clothing she would ever need.

But she wanted more than that now. She wanted Basil.

She tore the rest of the strip of cloth free. "You're going to be there, got it? We'll fetch my siblings together, and we're going to be a family, and you'll be the best big brother ever. Got it?"

Basil gave a small nod, his mouth quirking. "Got it."

Meg pressed a wad of the torn shirt to his injury, pressing hard enough to earn a cry of pain from Basil. Gritting her teeth to ignore his pain, Meg wrapped strips of fabric around his waist. His skin felt far too warm when her fingers brushed against his stomach, then his back, as she wound the scraps of shirt around him. He moaned, curling in on himself, as she tied the bandage as tightly as she could.

What was taking Hermia and Lysander so long? How hard was it to find one flower?

Basil pressed his hand to his stomach again, gasping in ragged breaths.

Meg rested her hands on top of his. She should distract him. Keep him talking. And she knew just the way to do that. "What are healers like here in the Fae Realm? Will they use magic to heal you?"

"Yes, and the antidote. It will take both. Magical poison takes a magical antidote." Basil tilted his head toward her, his eyes fluttering open for a moment before he squeezed them shut again.

That was a far shorter lecture than normal. Not a good sign.

"We got it!" Hermia's voice snapped Meg's head up as Hermia and Lysander dashed from the darkness, hands clasped. In her free hand, Hermia clutched two white flowers. Each flower was as big as a dinner plate with long, flopping petals and a gold interior coloring.

Basil's eyes flickered open again, and he pushed onto an elbow again, mouth twisting. He held out his hand, and Hermia plucked one of the flower heads from its stem and dropped it onto Basil's palm.

Without so much as a second's hesitation, Basil stuffed the whole thing in his mouth, his cheeks puffing out from such a large bite. He swallowed, grimaced, and swallowed again. "Ugh, that tastes awful."

"As long as it helps, I'll keep stuffing you full of them until we can get you to a healer." Meg took the other flower from Hermia. While Hermia seemed more reliable than most of the other fae, Meg felt better personally holding onto the flower that would keep Basil alive.

This time when Basil pushed himself upright, he managed to get all the way into a sitting position. His eyes still shone with a feverish light, but at least he could keep them open.

Meg glanced from him to Hermia and Lysander. "What's the plan now?"

Basil sucked in a breath, then held out his hand as if asking for help to pull him to his feet. "We still have to find Helena and Demetrius, rescue them from the love flower, then rescue Nick Bottom and Queen Titania, and hope all of that fixes the rift."

"No, first we need to get you to a healer." Meg gripped

Basil under the shoulder as Lysander took his hand. Together, they hauled Basil to his feet.

Basil looped one arm over Meg's shoulders, then the other over Lysander's. "We're closer to the Court of Revels. They might have a healer, but I doubt it. That Court's cruel streak doesn't sit well with a lot of healers. But I know there will be healers in the Court of Knowledge. Our Court has an agreement with the Order of Healers. They don't have a Court of their own, but they train in our Court, and that gives us a close alliance. And the quickest way back to the Court of Knowledge is to use the Anywhere Door in King Oberon and Queen Titania's palace."

Yep, he was back to lecturing. He must be feeling better.

Still, Meg wasn't taking no for an answer on this. Someone else could save the Fae Realm. Right now, Meg's priority was saving Basil.

## CHAPTER 17

*B*asil leaned on Meg and Lysander, trying to ignore the burning pain clawing its way from the pit of his stomach up into his chest, down into his legs, and into his arms. Even with the flower dulling his pain and lending him strength, the pain was worse than anything he'd ever experienced before.

Meg's lower jaw jutted in that stubborn look of hers. "Fine. We'll fix Nick Bottom and the queen on our way to the Anywhere Door. But I'm not letting you wander all over this forest with poison working its way through your veins, even with that fancy magic flower. Hermia and Lysander can find Helena and Demetrius."

"No need to find us!" A moment later, Helena strode from the shadows of the surrounding forest, gripping Demetrius's arm. He clasped her hand, looking down at her with a look of pure adoration.

There was something about that look. Basil didn't know a lot about love, but something in Demetrius's gaze still seemed…off.

Puck bounded from the forest. "Librarian Basil! I found them! And look, they are all better!"

Basil glanced from Demetrius and Helena, then focused on Puck, trying to give him a stern glare. "Puck, did you actually use the antidote nectar?"

"Well, about that…" Puck gestured to Helena and Demetrius. "Look at them. They're happy. They're meant to be together. What's the harm?"

Helena's gaze flicked between Basil and Puck. "What are you talking about?"

Basil withdrew his arm from Lysander's shoulders, then from Meg's. When Meg glanced up at him, he smiled and pointed toward the tree where she had stashed the rest of the antidote flowers. "We'll need one of those."

She nodded and hurried across the clearing. Hermia tugged Lysander to the side, as if understanding that Helena would need space for this discussion. Demetrius just stood there, gazing at Helena and smiling, his eyes empty. Puck, of course, didn't budge. He looked ready to start eating snacks while watching whatever happened next.

Basil limped a few steps closer to Helena, waiting until she met his gaze. "Puck used a love spell on you, Demetrius, Hermia, and Lysander."

"That explains what happened tonight." Helena shifted, glancing to Demetrius. "He's still under the spell, isn't he?"

"Yes." Basil worked to keep his breathing even. Ugh, the basilisk poison hurt.

Helena worried her lower lip. "Are you sure it would be so bad, if we left him like this? He loves me now."

Basil could tell her about the rift and how fixing what Puck had done would hopefully stop the monsters.

But that wasn't what Helena needed right now. Her problems with Demetrius had started long before tonight.

Gently, Basil rested a hand on her shoulder and gave it a

squeeze. "Helena, I'm your friend, and I say this as a friend. This isn't love, and you deserve better than a fake version caused by a magical flower."

"All I have ever wanted was for him to love me. He used to. And then he didn't, and it hurt so much." Helena sniffed, swiping at her face as tears trickled from her eyes. "What if he doesn't love me when the spell is broken?"

"Then he really wasn't the person for you." Basil kept his tone lowered, gentle. "Perhaps that is what you were supposed to learn through the Revel. That it is time to move on."

That was what the Revel had shown him, years ago, even if it had taken him until now to realize it.

"Easy for you to say." Helena gave a teary, bitter laugh. "You just snatched a mate, and that was that."

"Yes, I snatched Meg, and that's why I know this fake love isn't what you want." Basil glanced down to Meg as she eased to his side, clutching the antidote flowers. She gave him a smile back, not interrupting. Just lending support. Basil forced himself to turn back to Helena. "I fell in love with Meg when I learned to appreciate her for who she is, not who I wanted her to be. And that's the kind of love you want, Helena. You want a mate who will see *you*—the real you— and will love the person he sees. Not just a hazy, spelled version that would make him fall in love with the first girl he looked at."

Meg's fingers slipped into Basil's, holding tight.

Helena gave another sniff and gazed at Demetrius for one long moment. Then, she straightened her shoulders and nodded. "You're right. Of course you're right. You always were the wisest of all of us."

"Meg, can you restrain him?" Basil took a step toward Demetrius, his legs shaking beneath him. He wasn't sure he had the strength to lift his arms high enough to administer the flower's nectar.

Helena shook her head. "No. Let me. It should be me."

Meg held out one of the antidote flowers. When Helena took the flower, something unspoken passed between them.

Still crying silent tears, Helena turned to Demetrius. She smiled through her tears and wrapped her arms around his neck.

He smiled, mumbling her name.

Helena pressed her mouth to Demetrius's. He closed his eyes, embracing her. Sobbing, Helena lifted the white flower, then squeezed one drop onto each of Demetrius's eyelids.

After a moment, he froze, blinked, and pulled away from Helena. The passionate, empty look dropped from his face. "Helena? What's going on?"

"We'll explain later." Meg held both the remaining antidote flowers and the second strengthening flower in one hand, then tucked herself beneath Basil's arm once again. "There's a rift. Lots of monsters. Basil's dying. We need to get to the Court of Revels. Long story. Let's keep moving."

Meg started to march in one direction, but Basil steered her slightly more to the left. He couldn't say how he knew that was the right direction. Perhaps it was the magic of the Tanglewood.

As they passed the clearing, vines and roots had already twined over the body of the basilisk.

While the Library had a need to protect those inside, the Tanglewood was ancient and above the petty squabbles of fae and monsters. It might even allow monsters to roam its borders, as heroes slaying monsters were a part of the enchantment of a forest like the Tanglewood. It certainly wouldn't step in to help, besides rendering minor aid such as giving Meg the branch. But now that the basilisk was dead, the Tanglewood didn't want the body cluttering up its pristine forest floor.

Lysander, Hermia, Helena, and Demetrius fell into step behind them, not complaining at Basil's slow, limping pace.

Puck had disappeared, and Basil didn't have the strength to worry about where he had gone or what additional trouble he was causing.

As they walked, Basil only caught snatches of the conversation behind him. Apologies. Forgiveness for all the pain of not just that night, but for the past few months since Hermia's father tried to arrange her marriage. A heart-to-heart between Helena and Demetrius where they agreed to rebuild their relationship as friends and see what happened from there.

Perhaps it was Basil's imagination or the poison muddling his brain, but the pressing darkness eased. Had part of the rift been closed now that the four had been saved and the magic of the Revel restored? Basil hoped so. It would be nice if they didn't run into any more monsters. He wasn't in any shape for more fighting that night.

Meg remained silent, her expression taut. She gripped him around the waist, her steps steady and firm, as she hauled him along with forceful determination. As if she would keep him alive by sheer willpower, if that was what it took.

The farther they walked, the more Basil's legs shook. He gasped harder, the burning in his gut growing worse until tears streamed down his face unbidden.

Meg's arm tightened around his back. "We need to stop and let you rest."

"No." Basil swiped his sleeve over his forehead, and the fabric came away damp with sweat. "No time."

"But moving this much will speed up the poison." Meg

studied his face, her forehead furrowed. She held up her handful of flowers. "Do you need the second one?"

He could feel the burning spreading through him, leaving a strange numbness in its wake. But he shook his head. "Not yet."

He had to keep pushing forward. Earlier, he'd thought himself ready to die.

But he wasn't. He had too much to live for. Meg. Her siblings that he had yet to meet. The Library. Buddy. Hermia, Lysander, Helena, and Demetrius. Shoot, even Puck with his mischievous mayhem. They were his family. All of them.

For so long, Basil had thought himself alone. He'd mourned the loss of his parents. Mourned that he didn't have any siblings or family to call his own. All while he'd had a family right under his nose.

Meg was right. He wasn't the most observant fae in the realm.

"What you said back there. To Helena." Meg kept her head down as she trudged onward. "It was very nice. And sweet. And I like you for just who you are too. I thought you should know that."

"Meg…" His mind was going fuzzy, and his knees buckled.

She staggered as more of his weight fell onto her. "All right. Time for that second flower."

He managed a nod and didn't resist as she plucked the flower and shoved it at his face, popping the flower into his mouth like he was a child. He might have protested, but his free hand had started shaking. It was a struggle just to chew. Swallow. Chew some more. Swallow both the flower and the bile rushing up his throat.

"How far are we from the Court of Revels?" Meg's grip tightened on him.

He raised his head, trying to gather the strength to

answer. But Meg was looking over her shoulder, toward the others.

"We're not even halfway there." Hermia's voice was low, strained.

"Perhaps we can find more of those flowers? Will that be enough to get Basil to the Court of Revels?" Meg struggled back to her feet, dragging Basil along with her.

He tottered, trying not to put too much weight on her.

"Lysander and I can take turns carrying him." Demetrius stepped forward, reaching for Basil. "That will speed up our progress."

He was slowing them down. But he didn't want to be carried. He wanted to be that strong, fae warrior Meg had envisioned. He wasn't even sure why that was so important to him right at that moment. Even with the flower, his head was spinning.

Was that clopping noise he heard real or imagined? It didn't sound like his heartbeat or a ringing in his ears.

Then Meg and the others turned, and Buddy appeared out of the shadows. He favored his right front leg, but his head was up, his ears pricked forward. He nudged Basil with a nose. "You look awful."

"I feel awful." Basil buried a hand in Buddy's shaggy mane, then he sagged against Buddy's neck.

"I brought your talking equine companion to you! Aren't I helpful?" Puck's voice came from near Basil's elbow, but he didn't have the strength to lift his head to look at the sprite.

"Yes, you are very helpful." Meg's voice was warm, though her hand felt strangely cold against Basil's skin. "Let's get you onto Buddy."

He must have blacked out for a moment because the next thing he knew, he was sitting on Buddy's back, swaying with the rhythm of Buddy's footsteps and Meg's arms holding him in place.

The ride through the forest blurred.

Next thing Basil truly remembered, they were stepping out of the Tanglewood into a more open, glade-like forest. Glowing, hand-sized pixies darted between the trees and hovered among the branches. Nymphs and fauns peeked between the ferns and around the tree trunks before ducking back into hiding. A pall filled this forest, punctuated by the occasional scream of terror, instead of the giggles and frolicking that normally filled this court.

He rested his arm over Meg's around his waist, ignoring the renewed surge of pain. "Welcome to the Court of Revels."

## CHAPTER 18

*M*eg couldn't help but stare wide-eyed at the court unfolding around them. Those fae that dared step into view wore scanty outfits made of flowers or leaves. More flowers and leaves wove through the messy strands of their hair. Sprites like Puck bounded along the branches or scurried through the ferns.

Before them rose a tall cliff with jutting ledges. Tall trees arched over the space, forming a full canopy that looked like a grand hall of a castle, for all that it was an outdoor space.

But one of those black, twisting holes tore through the middle, wide and gaping and far larger than the rifts that had sliced through the Court of Knowledge. Something stalked in its depths, about to pour out to terrorize this court.

They hadn't seen any more signs of the rift on their way here. Perhaps the rest of it really had closed, once the problems with Hermia, Lysander, Helena, and Demetrius had been put to right.

A lion-shaped monster prowled from the rift. Long, glinting claws dug into the moss with each step.

With a shout, a horde of fauns wielding spears dashed

from around the trees. They surged toward the monster, swarming it.

A portly man dressed in a golden leaf loincloth and a golden crown, also made of leaves, raced behind the fauns, his head high and shouting orders as if he was pretending to be the leader, for all it seemed the fauns ignored his orders as they fought the monster.

"My King Oberon!" Puck shouted and dashed into the fray, nimbly dodging around the fauns' legs.

The fae man in the gold loincloth glanced up, then left the fight to stroll toward Meg, Basil, Buddy, and the others.

As he approached, Meg got a better look at him. The leaves forming his loincloth were real gold. His shoulders were broad. His chest was puffed out with bulging muscles, which looked off above the fae king's paunch hanging over the waistband of his loincloth. His curly brown hair would have been handsome, if each curl hadn't been so perfectly styled that they were waxy and stiff.

The man's face had the chiseled, devastatingly handsome look that was everything Meg had always imagined a fae lord would look like. Except that, like his hair, his face was almost too perfect. An exaggerated version of male beauty. Too chiseled jaw. Too defined cheekbones.

Could fae magically alter themselves somehow? Because if Meg were to guess, this fae man didn't always look like this. He definitely had magic done in some shape or form.

King Oberon spread his arms in what was probably supposed to be a magnanimous gesture. "Librarian Balsa! You have come to my summons!"

"It's Basil. But would the fool remember that? No," Buddy mumbled under his breath, low enough that Meg didn't think King Oberon would be able to hear. Thankfully.

Still, Meg couldn't fault Buddy. She was struggling to resist the urge to roll her eyes. She didn't know a lot about dealing with royalty, but sassing them probably wasn't wise. Especially not someone as unhinged as King Oberon.

Basil slid from Buddy's back, gripping the pony's mane as he swayed. "We have the antidote flower to close the rift and stop the monsters. Please take us to Queen Titania and Nick Bottom, if it pleases Your High Majesty."

Meg eased under Basil's other arm. He should be headed for the Anywhere Door, not worrying about this mess.

King Oberon's jaw hardened. As if, now that they were here to help, he was going to dig in his heels rather than admit his mistakes.

A second monster slithered from the rift. Another three-headed snake.

Hermia stepped forward, gripping the still bloody ax. Meg had been too focused on Basil to see her pick it up as they were leaving the clearing. Hermia gave a fierce smile as she passed Meg. "We'll help the Court of Revels fight off the monsters. You and Basil can see to King Oberon."

As Hermia and the others raced past, joining the fauns in attacking the monsters, Meg was sure they had taken the easier job.

"Your Majesty." Basil's voice was stronger, and he held his head high as he faced the king of the Court of Revels. "The monsters won't stop until we close the rift, and the rift won't close until we fix what has been done. Please."

Meg clenched her fist tightly, holding her breath. King Oberon was a few nuts shy of a full tree, but surely even he could see this was the only course of action.

King Oberon held Basil's gaze for a long moment, then a broad smile crossed his face. "Yes, of course, Librarian Balsam. Follow me."

"Thank you, Your Majesty." Basil took a step, nearly going to his knees as his legs buckled.

Meg pulled him upright. She was strong, but Basil's weight was a struggle.

Buddy gave a snort, but he didn't mutter anything under his breath as he started forward, supporting Basil. Meg could only be thankful that Buddy was showing some sensible restraint. The last thing Basil needed was for them to get kicked out of this court before they had a chance to use the Anywhere Door to get home.

King Oberon led the way deeper into the woodland palace. They followed the ridge of rock as it curved, the arching trees providing a semblance of a wall and roof. Fae peeked over the rims of the cliff and the ledges, their eyes wide. Most likely hiding in terror.

Meg couldn't blame them. She hadn't realized how much of a comfort it had been, knowing Queen Hippolyta's warrior women were there to step into the battle. The Court of Revels didn't have that. And these scantily clad, party-loving fae were hardly prepared for a war against monsters.

A war their own king and queen caused by their squabbles.

As they rounded a bend, a larger nook in the rock wall came into view. Small waterfalls cascaded down the cliff on either side of the ledge, forming a shining pool at the base. Gobs of ostentatious flowers bloomed from the trailing moss. Moss and vines provided something almost like a canopy around and over the ledge, creating a version of privacy. From inside the bower came the sounds of giggles.

King Oberon's mouth pressed into a tight line, his eyes flashing with heat.

Since his back was turned to her, Meg rolled her eyes this time. It wasn't like King Oberon had any right to be jealous when he was the one who caused this situation in the first place with his enchanted love flower.

King Oberon held out a hand. "Give me the antidote. I will deal with my wife."

Meg glanced to Basil. She wasn't going to let go of the flower until Basil said it was all right. She trusted Basil's judgment. Not King Oberon's.

Basil gave a nod, the gesture swaying his entire body.

Meg peeled her fingers off the last two flowers. She held out one, keeping the last one in reserve. If needed, it should be enough to save both Nick Bottom and Queen Titania, if King Oberon failed.

King Oberon climbed a set of worn steps in the cliff and disappeared inside the bower.

A moment later, Nick Bottom, his donkey-ears flapping, came hurtling through the vines and over the side of the ledge. The drop was only fifteen or twenty feet, and he rolled on the moss, unhurt. He sat up, blinking owlishly, his face still lit with some rapturous glow. His shirt hung unbuttoned, though he still wore his trousers.

Meg let go of Basil and hurried over to Nick. The donkey-headed fae man just sat there, gazing upward and muttering under his breath something about dreams and beauty and some poetic nonsense. He didn't resist as Meg dripped nectar into first one eye, then the other.

From the ledge above, King Oberon was also murmuring something, too low for Meg to hear.

"I have had a dream past the wit of fae to say what dream it was." Nick Bottom gave a sigh, then flopped onto his back, still gazing upward with a dazed expression.

Meg jabbed her finger at Bottom, glancing back to Basil. "Is he all right? Or should I dose him again?"

"No, that's just Nick Bottom. I think." Basil shrugged, then nearly sank to his knees again. Only his grip on Buddy's mane kept him upright.

Meg took a step toward him. He wasn't well. They had

delivered the flowers to the Court of Revels and rescued Bottom. Whatever happened now with Queen Titania was King Oberon's problem.

A scream pierced the air before a strident female voice rang from the ledge above.

Several nymphs and fauns darted from a hidden nook, gripped Bottom, and dragged him behind Buddy as if to keep the dazed fae man out of sight, before they dove back into their hiding spots.

Meg hurried back to Basil's side and glanced up just as King Oberon fled back down the stairs, followed by a blonde-haired female fae. She was also an exaggerated version of beauty, with thick, wavy blonde hair down to her over-sized rear end, waifishly tiny waist, and ample bosom barely covered by two strategically placed gold leaves. She also wore a golden leaf loincloth and crown like King Oberon's.

Meg was becoming increasingly convinced that leaves made for a very insufficient clothing option. The Court of Revels should really rethink their fashion.

She leaned closer to Basil and whispered, "Scrambled squirrels, what does this Court have against clothing?"

Basil snorted, then pressed a hand to his stomach. "Don't make me laugh."

"Don't worry." Buddy gave a low snort. "In a few moons, fashions will change, and they will be so overstuffed, over-dressed, bejeweled, and beribboned that you will hardly be able to tell there's a fae under all that fabric."

Queen Titania gave another shriek and stomped after King Oberon. "How dare you! Ingrate! Slime! Poltroon! See if I let you into my bower again!"

King Oberon spun on his heel, facing his wife. "Now, Titania, let's not overreact. It was just a little prank."

"Overreact! A prank!" Queen Titania descended into a

long tirade peppered with what sounded like the fae version of swearing. Based on the way King Oberon flinched away from her, this wasn't the first time she'd unleashed her tongue on him.

At this point, Meg wasn't sure which of the two she was rooting for. Neither of them, honestly. These were two selfish people in an unhealthy relationship, too busy hurting each other and themselves to even realize they were miserable.

She would have pitied them, if their marital strife hadn't been delaying help for Basil.

Meg marched forward, fists clenched. Enough was enough. She had fought monsters. Her husband was dying. And it was all the fault of these two. "Hey!" When neither of them stopped their argument, Meg drew in a deeper breath. "Enough!"

Both King Oberon and Queen Titania glanced to her, going silent.

"Look. I don't know what you're arguing about, and right now, I don't care." Meg planted her feet, hands on her hips. She wasn't going to back down, even if these two were a king and queen. "Basil was bitten by a basilisk. He needs to get back to the Court of Knowledge as quickly as possible. I can't lose him. He's my home. So if you don't show me your Anywhere Door right this minute, I'm going to set your loin-cloths on fire. Understand?"

King Oberon gaped, looking like he'd swallowed an especially slimy frog.

Strangely, Queen Titania's eyes softened, and she placed a hand over her heart. "Aww. That's so sweet and romantic." She glanced at King Oberon. "They are in love. Love is so beautiful."

When King Oberon glanced down at her, it was as if all

the screeching of a moment ago was forgotten. "Yes, my honeyed flower."

The next moment, the two of them locked in a passionate embrace.

Meg glanced over her shoulder at Basil. He shrugged. Next to him, Buddy shook his head in his version of an eyeroll.

As the minute stretched into two and the couple showed no sign of stopping, Meg cleared her throat. When that didn't work, she shouted, "Hey! Kiss later. Basil is dying."

King Oberon straightened his crown as he stepped away from Queen Titania, his tone normal as if he wasn't embarrassed in the least. "Librarian Ballyrags, you and your fellow librarians have done this Court a great service. I will personally provide an escort to return all of you to King Theseus's Court."

"We both will." Queen Titania rested her hand on King Oberon's arm, giving him a starry smile. "We should offer our felicitations to King Theseus and Queen Hippolyta on their upcoming nuptials."

"Yes, we should welcome them to their new happy state of matrimony." King Oberon's heated gaze remained focused on Queen Titania.

Frolicking felines, this was worse than herding cats. Meg opened her mouth to shout again, but King Oberon and Queen Titania swept forward at a pace that would have looked regal and dignified, if they hadn't been wearing leaves for clothing.

With a shrug, Meg hauled a dreamy Nick Bottom to his feet and pushed him in front of her. Basil was barely conscious, slumped against Buddy.

His eyes worried, Buddy bent, lowering his front half so that Meg could flop Basil across his back. While she huffed and puffed at Basil's limp weight, Bottom just stood there, staring off into the sky and muttering to himself.

When Basil was situated, Buddy heaved to his feet, giving a grunt as he placed weight on his right front leg.

Gripping Bottom's sleeve and placing a hand on Basil's back to keep him from sliding off, Meg started after King Oberon and Queen Titania once again.

When they arrived at the great hall, the black rift was gone, though the bodies of the monsters lay bloody and gruesome on the moss. The fauns, as well as Hermia, Lysander, Helena, and Demetrius, gazed about with weapons still clutched in their hands.

King Oberon opened a door set into an arching set of trees. The opening showed the white floor and marbled hall of the Court of Knowledge.

Meg barely noticed as Demetrius and Helena took custody of Bottom while Lysander steadied Basil on Buddy's back. Hermia put her arm around Meg's shoulders, lending strength.

She stepped through the Door in an exhausted haze. Fae rushed forward, some taking charge of Basil and Buddy. Lysander, Hermia, Demetrius, and Helena were swept up in a rush of richly dressed fae, their noble parents most likely. King Oberon and Queen Titania stood before King Theseus and Queen Hippolyta, and whatever they said had King Theseus shifting and Queen Hippolyta gripping her sword as if she were thinking about stabbing them.

The first rays of sunlight speared through the windows far above.

It was morning. Midsummer Night was over.

## CHAPTER 19

*B*asil struggled through a fog of darkness and pain. Sensation came slowly. First, soft padding beneath his back. Then, something soft and warm beneath his head. Fingers ran through his hair, sending tingles across his scalp and down his back.

"That feels good," he mumbled, turning his head to a more comfortable position.

"You're awake." Meg's voice came from just above his head, and his pillow shifted.

"Mostly awake." Basil didn't yet feel strong enough to open his eyes. It was rather nice lying there. He might just go back to sleep.

"Enough sleeping." Buddy snorted near Basil's ear, a moment before something warm and wet and slimy swiped over Basil's ear, leaving behind gooey saliva.

"Ew." Basil snapped his eyes open. He tried to lift his hand to swipe the pony spit off his ear, but his hand was strangely heavy.

He glanced down and discovered his hand was gripped in Meg's, his other hand resting beneath their clasped ones. The thin gold line around each of their wrists from their marriage binding glinted in the sunlight streaming from somewhere overhead. He was missing both his librarian coat and shirt, though his stomach was swathed in bandages. When he swung his gaze up, he realized his head rested in Meg's lap, her face only a few inches above his. She smiled down at him, her eyes teary.

Buddy's head craned over Meg's, peering down at Basil. "Took you long enough to wake. The healers patched you up ages ago. They even had time to fix up my leg. Not to mention you completely missed King Theseus and Queen Hippolyta's wedding. Oh, and Hermia and Lysander also got hitched, and even Helena and Demetrius are back to being friends. Seems the Revel did its job and brought them all together as they were supposed to be."

"I still think you fae are crazy in your marriage traditions, you know that?" Meg shook her head, her fingers pausing on his forehead. "Even if everything worked out all right for us, in the end."

"It did, at that." Basil squeezed her fingers, smiling up at her. Her hair tumbled over her shoulders, smudges of dirt and blood streaking her face. Her clothes also still bore the signs of battle. "How long was I out?"

"Most of the day. It is late afternoon now." Meg's eyes lifted to something off to the side.

He craned his neck, following her gaze. He lay in a hall of the castle, along with rows of other cots filled with wounded. Fae from the Order of Healers moved between the wounded.

At the far end of the room, King Theseus and Queen Hippolyta knelt next to a cot, speaking with the injured female fae lying there. A few rows away, Head Librarian Marco was also moving between the wounded. Standing next to the door, two of Queen Hippolyta's swordmaidens kept watch.

"Seeing the Court of Revels made me even more thankful you are a part of the Court of Knowledge." Meg gave a shudder, her arms gripping Basil tighter. "So thankful you have sensible monarchs like King Theseus, and now Queen Hippolyta."

Queen Hippolyta looked up, then tapped King Theseus on the arm. Together, they worked their way across the room, heading toward Basil and Meg.

Basil tried to push himself into a sitting position—he was going to be facing his king and queen after all—but he couldn't manage it. Pain shot through his middle, and he groaned.

Meg pushed him back down. "Lie still. You're still healing and weak. They'll understand if you can't give them a proper bow."

King Theseus and Queen Hippolyta reached Basil's pallet, and King Theseus knelt. "Librarian Basil, Meg of the Human Realm, I am told that I have you to thank for saving my Court from the rift to the Realm of Monsters."

"Meg did most of it." Basil wasn't sure where he should look. It seemed disrespectful to meet his king's gaze.

"Yes. We heard of her bravery." Queen Hippolyta smiled, then nodded to Meg. "You have shown strength worthy of my swordmaidens. If you should wish to join their ranks, I would give my blessing. Now that our Courts are joined, you could be one of the swordmaidens stationed here."

Basil's stomach clenched, but he clamped his mouth shut. This was Meg's decision. He would miss having her at his side in the Library, but if she wanted to train and become a swordmaiden, then he wouldn't stand in her way. Queen Hippolyta was right. She had shown the courage of a warrior during Midsummer Night.

Meg glanced from Queen Hippolyta to the guarding warrior women before finally focusing on Basil.

He held her gaze, then gave her a nod.

She drew in a deep breath and faced Queen Hippolyta. "Thank you for your kind offer, Your Majesty, but I would like to continue working in the Library with Basil. Though, I wouldn't mind receiving training from your warriors. It seems even the job of assistant librarian is a dangerous one around here."

Queen Hippolyta smiled, the expression lighting her face. "I already intend to make sure anyone in the Court of Knowledge who wants training shall receive it."

"If you are looking for more women to train, I believe Hermia would also make a worthy addition. She hacked the head off a basilisk last night." Meg's mouth quirked.

"Yes, Hermia. I have been told she is little but fierce." Queen Hippolyta glanced at King Theseus, the two of them seeming to exchange a silent, inside joke.

After a moment, King Theseus turned to Basil. "And you, Basil. What reward do you wish to receive for your valiant efforts last night?"

A reward. Basil's mind raced. This was his chance to ask for everything he had ever wanted. A promotion to Master Librarian. No more taking orders from Master Librarian Domitius. No more doing all the work for nobles who had just taken the job of assistant librarian for the temporary status.

Yet...Basil swung his gaze up to Meg. He knew what he had to ask.

"Your Majesty, my wife Meg has siblings back in the Human Realm." This time, Basil gathered enough courage to meet his king's gaze. He had intended to ask for more resources after he had brought Meg's family here, but it would be even better if he could get King Theseus's permission beforehand. "They are orphans and alone. I would like your blessing to bring them here so that Meg and I can raise them, and I respectfully request more of the Court's resources in order to properly care for them."

"You have my blessing to bring them here and care for them. You also have my word that I will bind them to the Court." King Theseus glanced to Queen Hippolyta. When she gave a nod, he waved to the swordmaidens standing behind them. "I will provide an escort for you to retrieve them tonight. You will wish to take advantage of the magic still being high and the barrier thin, especially when taking several humans back with you into our realm."

"Thank you, Your Majesty." Basil squeezed Meg's fingers. He would have to explain exactly what King Theseus was offering once they were alone. By binding her siblings to the Court, they would be as much a part of the Court of Knowledge as Basil or Meg were. They would have a layer of protection that Basil alone would not have been able to give them.

King Theseus pushed to his feet, took Queen Hippolyta's hand, then strolled away.

Head Librarian Marco quickly took their place, his white beard a good foot shorter than it had been the day before, the ends blackened and singed. "Good to see you both survived the night. It was a Midsummer Night for the history books, and I should know. I've written an entire shelf of them."

"We're glad to see you alive as well, sir." Basil relaxed against Meg. "How is the Library? Has the rift been fully healed?"

"Yes. Thanks to the two of you." Marco reached into an inner pocket of his gold-trimmed librarian coat. He yanked out a green librarian coat. "I've heard your old one was no longer salvageable. But…" Marco's forehead furrowed in an exaggerated frown. "I think this is the wrong color. Actually, I know it is the wrong color."

"Wrong color, sir?" What was Head Librarian Marco talking about? Basil couldn't process this puzzle.

Marco flapped the coat, and in a blink, the fabric changed from dark green to black. Marco grinned and held out the coat toward Basil. "There. This looks better."

"But...but that's..." Maybe it was the basilisk poison, but Basil's brain felt muddled. Surely this couldn't mean what he thought it meant.

"A master librarian's coat, yes." Head Librarian Marco regarded Basil, his grin fading into something solemn. "A long overdue promotion. It seems I was short one master librarian, now that I have assigned Domitius to the vacant position overseeing our outpost library in Bog's Bottom."

Bog's Bottom was even more of a backwater than Bog's End, situated at the border the Court of Knowledge shared with the Swamp Court. Domitius would loathe it.

And Basil would take up the job he had always dreamed about and never think about Domitius again, if he didn't have to.

Basil pushed into a sitting position, then all the way to his feet, leaning on Meg and Buddy. After waiting for a moment for his head to stop spinning, he took the coat from Marco. "Thank you, sir."

Basil needed Meg's help to shrug into it, the thick fabric settling against the bare skin of his shoulders.

Smiling, she smoothed the lapels over his chest. "Master Librarian Basil. I like the sound of that."

"So do I." He clasped his hand over hers. This was probably the moment he was supposed to say something romantic, but his brain just kept fizzing and swirling.

"Wait, I think there's something more in this pocket." Marco withdrew a second librarian coat. This one was dark green and tailored in a slimmer, feminine silhouette. "If

177

you're going to be working at Basil's side, we should make it official, I think."

Meg's mouth fell open, and she reached for the coat, her fingers stopping short. "But I can't even read."

"While reading is an important source of knowledge—and one of which I heartily approve—it is not the only source." Head Librarian Marco grinned once again. "Here in the Court of Knowledge, we are purveyors of all kinds of knowledge. You, Meg, have shown yourself a knowledgeable source of practical matters. For that, I name you Assistant Librarian of Sensible Things, or whatever title you prefer."

"But…" Meg glanced from the coat to Basil, her eyes wide. "Surely that isn't a real thing."

"It is if I say it is." Head Librarian Marco sounded supremely satisfied as he smoothed his singed beard over his chest. "Our book repair room is in desperate need of someone to devote attention to it. And, while we have done well in providing training to healers and artists, we have long neglected the tradesmen and farmers. It is time they had an assistant librarian of their own."

Basil squeezed Meg's fingers. "You're perfect for this."

"But I don't know everything about farming." Meg's voice rose, as if more panicked at the thought of this new job than at all the monsters they'd faced during the night. "I just know about the few crops and animals we had on our farm before the drought. And I don't know anything about growing food or raising animals here in this realm."

"That's why you're starting out as an assistant librarian." Marco held out the librarian coat again, wagging it back and forth. "Part of your job will be gathering information in your field and learning what you don't know. When you become an expert, then you'll be promoted, just like Basil here."

A slow grin spread across Meg's face, and she took the coat.

As she pulled it on, something swelled inside Basil's chest, and his own grin felt like it would tear his face apart. For some reason, he felt far prouder watching Meg don that dark green librarian coat than when he'd put on his new black one.

Meg faced him, her eyes sparkling, the coat hugging her frame perfectly.

But before he could reach for her, Buddy stuck his head between them and snorted. "As proud as I am of both of you, a squad of swordmaidens just arrived and they are looking rather impatient. Save the romantic moment for later, got it?"

"Right." Basil met Meg's gaze over Buddy's shoulders. "Let's fetch your family."

## CHAPTER 20

*M*eg's heart hammered as she strode toward the ramshackle hut that had once been her home. It looked worse now than when she'd left with holes in the thatched roof and one side so rotted that the roof sagged and the wall was on the verge of collapse. Light shone through the cracks between the boards, pouring light into the surrounding darkness of night.

How much time had passed here in the Human Realm since she left? Or did the hut just look so dilapidated compared to her new House?

It had been a risk, but she and Basil had taken the time to return to the House—which had been safe and sound and shivering with happiness at their return—in order to wash and dress in clean clothes. She hadn't wanted to scare her siblings by showing up in monster-gore-drenched clothing.

Basil's hand tightened on hers, and she leaned into him, grateful for the comfort he provided. When she glanced at him, he gave her a smile, even if the tightness around his eyes showed how tired he was.

Buddy walked on her other side, a warm bulk beneath her hand.

Two of the swordmaidens marched ahead while two more strode behind them, silent and menacing.

As they neared the hut, the shadows of horses materialized out of nighttime gloom.

Meg gripped Basil's hand harder, picking up her pace. "We don't own any horses. Cullen and his henchmen are here."

Raised voices shattered the nighttime stillness, then a shriek.

Meg pulled away from Basil, dodged around the swordmaidens, and raced for the hut. She burst inside, the door knocking into one of the sharp-faced men that Cullen always had with him.

Cullen gripped Brigid's arm, Meg's sister squirming and wincing. The rest of Meg's siblings huddled in the corner with Sebastian standing in front of them, his fists clenched as if he thought he could take on Cullen and his four cronies all by himself.

For a silent moment, Brigid locked eyes with Meg. Then, she struggled and kicked at Cullen, her face twisting. "Meg! You need to get out of here!"

Cullen turned, a smile creeping onto his face. "Ah, Meg. Just in time. You are looking well. Very well."

Meg lifted her chin. Cullen no longer had any power over her. "Let her go."

"Are you offering yourself in her place?" Cullen's gaze swept over her with a calculating glint. "I might get enough for you to pay your family's debt. Maybe. I have expenses, you know, and the interest on your little excuse for a farm has built up considerably. It is a pity, but I am a businessman."

The sound of footsteps sounded just outside the door. It

gave Meg the courage to continue facing Cullen, her hands fisted at her sides. "No, you traffic in human lives under the guise of indentured servitude. But that ends today."

The four swordmaidens marched into the hut, followed by Basil. Buddy stuck his head inside for good measure.

Cullen's eyes widened, and he froze at the sight of the fierce warrior women. His four henchmen gaped and shifted away from both Cullen and from the swordmaidens, unwilling to face such fearsome warriors for Cullen's sake.

When a swordmaiden pressed her sword to Cullen's throat, he dropped Brigid's arm and raised his hands.

Brigid dashed to the rest of Meg's siblings, placing her hands on Viola's and Beatrice's shoulders. They all had wide eyes, as if they were nearly as terrified of the swordmaidens as Cullen was.

Meg stalked to Cullen, looking him in the eye. "You will never harm my family again."

Cullen gave a nod, but his eyes shifted away from her.

What was she supposed to do with him now? Her family would be safe, but what about all the innocent villagers left behind? They would still be at Cullen's mercy. Whatever momentary fear he felt now, he would forget it by morning.

Meg glanced over her shoulder to Basil. "What should I do with him?"

Basil studied Cullen, mouth pressed into a tight line.

"Actually…" Puck's voice came from the door a moment before he squirmed between Buddy's front legs and popped into the room. "I'll take him."

"Puck?" Meg eyed the little green sprite where he stood in the center of her family's hut in all his green-skinned, barely-clad glory. "What are you doing here?"

"Causing mischief, probably." Buddy shook his head, rolling his eyes as much as a pony could.

"I followed you, of course!" Puck smirked, hooking his

thumbs in his loincloth. "Now that King Oberon and Queen Titania are in love at the moment, I won't be needed until they go at it again. Following you to the Human Realm seemed much more fun."

"What…what is that thing? What's it saying?" For the first time, true terror shook through Cullen's voice. He backed away from the swordmaiden and Meg, holding his hands out in front of him. The four cronies edged toward the door, faces twisted in gaping horror.

As Puck took another bound into the room, Cullen scrambled backwards, pressing his back to the wall. "Get it away from me!"

"Give him to me." For a moment, Puck's face twisted into an expression of cruel glee. "I will repay your aid this past night by tormenting your tormentor."

Meg probably should feel bad, turning Puck loose on anyone, even her worst enemy.

But Cullen was the scum of the earth, selling men, women, and children into indentured servitude for his own profit. Perhaps this was the punishment he deserved.

"Very well." Meg nodded to Puck. Maybe her few days in the Fae Realm had changed her more than she'd thought.

When Puck flashed a many-toothed, sinister smile at Cullen, the man gave a very uncourageous shriek and made a break for the door, his henchmen several steps ahead of him.

Buddy stepped aside, letting the five men sprint past him.

"What fools these mortals are, thinking they can flee from me!" Puck bounded after them, giggling, as if it was all a big game. His high-pitched voice could be heard singing as he and his prey disappeared into the darkness, "Up and down, up and down, I will chase them up and down. I am feared in field and town. Run until the moon goes down."

After a moment, screams pierced the night, followed by Puck's maniacal cackling.

When Meg turned back to her siblings, they were all gaping at her. Right. They couldn't understand what Puck had said. And Puck had been at his most terrifying.

"Meg…" Brigid glanced from her to Basil and back. "What's going on? Who are these…people?"

Brigid's voice squeaked on the last word, as if she thought something horrible would happen if she said the word *fae* out loud.

"It's all right. Everything is going to be all right from now on." Meg hurried across the room and hugged her sister, then reached to embrace the rest of her siblings all at once. They felt so bony in her arms. Had she been this thin when Basil had snatched her only a few days ago?

"You were gone for so long." Beatrice wrapped her arms around Meg's waist, breaking into sobs.

"We thought you were never coming back." Viola hugged both Beatrice and Meg, also crying.

"How long was I gone?" Meg held her breath, not sure if she wanted to know the answer.

"Eight months." Sebastian's chin wobbled, even as he stood tall, pretending to be brave.

Only months, though far too close to the year deadline Meg had given them when she had left. It hurt, knowing her siblings had been worried about her for that long. For her, it had only been a few days.

"I know. But I'm here now. And you're all going to be safe." Meg glanced over her shoulder. The swordmaidens were quietly filing from the hut, but Basil still stood there, resting a hand on Buddy's neck. When he caught her gaze, he gave her a nod. Buddy blinked in a pony version of a wink.

Brigid's shoulders shook. Then tears were streaming down her face as she faced Meg, tipping her head toward Basil. She spoke in a lowered tone, as if thinking this wasn't something Basil should hear, though he wouldn't be able to understand Meg's family until they were bound to the Court. "Is that the fae lord you set out to marry? Is he going to pay off Cullen with faerie gold as you hoped?"

"Does he treat you right?" Sebastian eyed Basil, as if wondering if he needed to protect Meg from him.

Meg reached out and squeezed her brother's shoulder. "Basil has been very good to me. The best, actually."

Sebastian sent another searching look in Basil's direction, but he nodded.

Meg turned, still holding her family in her arms as best she could. "Everyone, this is my husband, Basil. He's a Master Librarian at a magic library."

Basil waved, but he didn't speak. Perhaps he realized it would be better if he kept his mouth shut until her siblings were bound to the Court and could understand what he was saying.

"And this is Buddy." Meg gestured toward the pony, who gave her the side-eye. "I mean, Sir Buddy the Magnificent. He is our talking pony companion and the most valiant steed I know."

That earned her a twitch of Buddy's ears and a satisfied nod.

Beatrice gazed at Buddy with something like love at first sight, tugging against Meg's grip as if she intended to rush over to the pony and give him a big hug.

"Basil has offered to do even better than pay off Cullen. We're taking all of you back to the Fae Realm to live with us." Meg smiled, embracing each of her siblings in turn. It felt so good to hold them all again, especially since she'd done exactly what she'd set out to do in rescuing them all from Cullen.

"Really?" Viola gaped up at her.

"We're all going to be snatched by faeries?" Brigid stared

at the door, as if she could see past Basil and Buddy to the swordmaidens waiting outside.

Meg touched Viola's arm to get her attention. "It's not as scary as it sounds. Well, some of the Courts, like Puck's Court, are bizarre, but Basil's Court is nice. We have a magic house that will provide all of us with nice clothes and as much food as you can eat. The Fae Realm is a little crazy, but it is beautiful, and you'll love it." Meg's voice choked as she met Basil's gaze across the room. "We're going home."

When he smiled, it sent tingles from her chest all the way down into her toes.

Home. With her family. With him.

It was all more wonderful than she ever could have imagined.

It was late by the time they all trooped back into the Fae Realm and traveled to the castle. There, King Theseus bound her siblings to the Court, and they were all invited to stay to watch Nick Bottom and the players put on their performance. Despite his obvious exhaustion, Basil still insisted that they stay, and Meg didn't have the heart to argue that he should rest when she saw her siblings' wonder and excitement.

Meg had never seen a play before, but she was pretty sure she wasn't supposed to snort with laughter at a tragedy where everyone dies. After everything that had happened in the past few days, it felt good to laugh.

By the time they strode through the Anywhere Door and stepped into the House, Basil was leaning most of his weight onto Meg, his steps unsteady.

She tightened her grip on him. "We shouldn't have stayed. You need to rest."

Basil quirked a tiny smile at her, though weary lines grooved his face. "It was worth it to hear your laugh."

Meg hauled him a few more steps into the house, making room for Buddy to trot through the Anywhere Door with Viola and Beatrice grinning and shrieking on his back. Sebastian and Brigid trailed after them, gazing about to take it all in.

As soon as all four of her siblings were inside and the Door closed, the entire House tilted and shook so violently that Meg had to cling to Buddy to keep herself and Basil upright.

"What was that?" Brigid braced herself against the wall.

Viola and Beatrice clung to Buddy with such a tight grip, it probably hurt. Sebastian clenched his fists, as if prepared to take on the magical House to protect his siblings.

"I warned you that the House was a little temperamental." Meg shook her head, transferred Basil's arm to Buddy's neck, then walked to the Anywhere Door, pulling it open. As expected, it showed the bathing grotto. "And it is especially picky about cleanliness. Who wants to wash first?"

Brigid pushed away from the wall next to the Door. "I will."

"The water is warm. And the House will fix up your dress while you're at it." Meg grinned, then gave her sister a push toward the Door.

Eventually, they all rotated through the bathing grotto and ate their first decent meal in years. The longer the night wore on, the more talkative and exuberant her siblings became, as if they had shed all the fear and pain of their old life along with the dirt they had scrubbed away.

When they were ready for bed, Meg showed each of her siblings their new rooms, ones that were identical to the room that the House had added for her.

Viola and Beatrice squealed in excitement at the

wardrobes and the fact each of them would have their own rooms. Sebastian tried to pretend he was nonchalant, but he was grinning ear to ear. Brigid immediately opened the wardrobe, her eyes brightening at the gorgeous dress that appeared there.

Finally, Meg stepped back through the Anywhere Door and shut it behind her. The main room felt oddly quiet, with only her, Basil, and Buddy in it.

Buddy clopped across the room, then rested the end of his nose on the top of her head. "I am never going to get another peaceful moment, am I?"

Meg reached up and patted Buddy's soft neck. "You love how they dote on you. Admit it."

"I appreciate that they know magnificence when they see it." Buddy took his head from on top of hers, turning toward his stall. "Now I'm going to bed. I have a feeling they will wake me up far too early for proper beauty sleep."

He flicked Meg with his tail as he clopped away, disappearing into his stall a moment later, both halves of the door shutting behind him.

That left Meg alone with Basil. He sprawled in a chair, leaning his head back, his eyelids drooping.

Meg strode to his side and rested a hand on his shoulder. "Come on. Let's get you to bed."

He nodded and held out a hand. It took all of her strength to pull him to his feet. He sagged against her as he managed two wobbling steps.

Meg grasped the handle of the Anywhere Door, willing it to open to Basil's bedroom.

When the Anywhere Door swung open, the room on the other side held a mish-mash of both Meg's and Basil's things. Two wardrobes filled one wall, one of them hanging open as she had left hers before leaving to go fight monsters on Midsummer Night. One of Basil's gray shirts lay on the floor.

At the far end of the room, a large sleeping nook was formed into the wall, big enough for two people.

Rancid rats, the House was far too invested in her and Basil's relationship. She groaned and leaned her head against the doorjamb.

Basil's grip around her shoulders tightened. "Sorry. The House decided…this is…if you aren't…I can sleep out here."

Meg pushed away from the jamb. This was fine. It wasn't that she was all that opposed to the idea, exactly. She just hadn't been expecting it, was all. "As far as my family is concerned, we've been married for eight months. And we are both too tired for this conversation right now. Let's get you to bed, and we can talk about what to do with the whole one bed, one room thing in the morning."

Right now, all she wanted to do was collapse into bed and sleep. She didn't care if that meant sharing a bed, since she was going to pass out like a milk-drunk cat no matter where she was.

"Sounds sensible." Basil pushed away from her, his tone flat, and he took a shaking step forward.

Meg could have groaned. She hadn't meant for him to take it as a dismissal. She hurried a step to catch up with him. "Don't worry. I fully intend to give you a kiss goodnight."

Basil turned toward her, straightening as if the thought of her kiss gave him strength. "Now that definitely sounds sensible."

"Exactly." Meg took Basil's arm to steady him, then tugged him all the way into the room.

She was already kissing him—or maybe he was kissing her—even before she pulled the Door shut behind her.

Perhaps it was her imagination, but she was positive she could hear the House quietly snickering.

Don't miss the next STOLEN BRIDES OF THE FAE book!

COLLECT THE ENTIRE STOLEN BRIDES OF THE FAE
SERIES!

Read these books in any order for swoon-worthy romance,
heart-stopping adventure, and guaranteed happily-ever-
afters!

You can find them all at www.stolenbrides.com

Thanks so much for reading *Stolen Midsummer Bride*! I hope Basil and Meg stole your heart the way they stole mine. If you loved the book, please consider leaving a review on Amazon or Goodreads. Reviews help your fellow readers find books that they will love.

If you want to learn about all my upcoming releases, get great book recommendations, and see a behind-the-scenes glimpse into my writing process, sign up for my newsletter and check out my website at www.taragrayce.com.

If you sign up for my newsletter, you'll receive a free novella, *Steal a Swordmaiden's heart.*

This novella is a prequel to *Stolen Midsummer Bride,* and tells the story of how King Theseus of the Court of Knowledge won the hand of Hippolyta, Queen of the Swordmaidens.

Sign up for my newsletter now

# ALSO BY TARA GRAYCE

## ELVEN ALLIANCE SERIES

Fierce Heart

War Bound

Death Wind

Troll Queen

Pretense

## STOLEN BRIDES OF THE FAE

Stolen Midsummer Bride

## A VILLAIN'S EVER AFTER

Bluebeard and the Outlaw

## PRINCESS BY NIGHT

Lost in Averell

# ACKNOWLEDGEMENTS

Thank you to everyone who made this release possible! To my writer friends, especially Molly, Morgan, Addy, Savannah, Sierra, and the entire Spinster Aunt gang for being so encouraging and helpful. Thanks especially to all the Stolen Brides authors—Emma Hamm, Sylvia Mercedes, S.M. Gaither, Angela Ford, Clare Sager, Kenley Davidson, and Sarah Wilson—for making this such a fun and encouraging project. I learned so much and grew as an author just by participating in this series!

Thanks also to all my family and friends who make this author life of mine possible. To my dad for being such a thorough and thoughtful early reader. To my mom for supporting me. To my sisters-in-law Alyssa and Abby for helping me to write romance. To my brothers for being everything brothers should be in all the best ways possible. To my friends: Bri, for getting my Shakespeare references; Paula, for making my books your late-night, baby-feeding company; and Jill, for trying out my book recommendations when I shove them at you. A special thanks to Marco for being such a good sport about the use of his name (the hazards of marrying a writer's best friend). To my proof-readers Tom, Mindy, and Deborah, thanks so much for helping to eradicate the typos as much as humanly possible. All of you guys are the best team an author could ask for!

Printed in Great Britain
by Amazon

63930711R00115